Make Believe

PADDLE CREEK DADDIES BOOK SIX

HJ WELCH

Make Believe
Paddle Creek Daddies Book Six

Copyright © 2024 by HJ Welch

Cover Design: Cate Ashwood
Cover Model: Stephen Crowe
Cover Photographer: Graham Martin @ Menart.co.uk

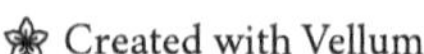 Created with Vellum

CHAPTER 1
Kadence

"Remind me again why we're here?"

I try not to whine. That's never a cute look. But as frat parties go, this is looking horribly straight from the outside. I can see a lot of football players and…you know…*dudes.*

My bestie, Jessie, chuckles and rubs my back. "Come on," he encourages me. "School's almost out for the summer, you've basically graduated, and we promised we'd go to as many of these things as possible as a bon voyage. I think the whole cheer squad is here. We'll have fun, I promise."

I tut and roll my eyes but allow myself to be ushered up the steps of the Alpha Zeta Kappa frat house. Jessie had a bit of a rocky start to his time with the Paddle Creek Kittens, and he has three more years of college yet with a lot of these people. If it's important to him, I'll make the effort.

But no one better try and talk sportsball at me. I am fully prepared to fake my death if necessary.

I met Jessie in his first semester because I make it a habit to seek out and befriend cute, kinky queers. I might be more or less done with college, but I'll be sticking around this tiny town for now at least because these people are my family.

They're the only family I've got.

I shake myself and take a second to remember that my sister isn't actually the worst human being. We just have very little in common, and for the last couple of years, she's been off wandering the earth, chasing her happiness in a different way. She's got yoga on a beach. I've got dick and tequila.

To each their own.

Mercifully, Jessie knows to grab my hand and pull us through the busy house directly to the kitchen to get our refreshment on. Waiting there is the tall, slim, and blond form of one of my other best friends I've made this year. I'm happier leaving campus knowing that Harper and Jessie will both still be studying together.

Selfishly, however, I know a little space from them is also necessary for my sanity. Don't get me wrong—I'm thrilled that they've both found their dream Daddies. Harper technically has *three* guys who Dom him in different ways, lucky bitch. But there are times when I find it hard to see just how sappy the two of them get.

Love is fine for other people. But there's only so much I can have it shoved down my throat. I don't do emotions. At least not deep and meaningful ones. Does snarky count as an emotion? I can do that plenty.

"Don't you both look fabulous?" Harper comments, already waiting with two cups of punch to thrust into our hands. I sniff it and he grins. "Don't worry. I already tested it. It's got a kick, but it's not going to erase that degree you just earned from your brain."

We laugh and tap our cups together in a toast. "To Kadence," Jessie says brightly.

I love how he'll often wear his kitten ear headbands out in public now, unafraid to show a bit of his true nature to the world at large. My kinky side is so completely separate from the rest of my life I'd never think of doing anything like that. But I still look pretty fucking gay in my tight leather pants and shimmery tank. Jessie's got a cute crop top on and denim shorts along with his ears, whereas Harper looks a little more sophisticated in a button-down open over a T-shirt. We're a bit of an eclectic bunch, but I feel nothing but warmth as we all drink together.

By the time I'm on my second cup, I start to think that maybe this party won't be so bad after all. Sometimes, I forget just how many of the football players are in fact gay, thanks to Coach Drevin being so out and proud. Consequently, a lot of the cheerleaders are also queer, and even a few of the basketball players.

It's kind of staggering to think about the knock-on effect Drevin has had on this small, kind of crappy town. It's most likely why he was able to get the job in the first place. I bet bigger colleges and universities balked at the idea of an out gay coach. But Paddle Creek isn't exactly renowned for anything much at all, so the dean was probably stoked to have someone of such caliber step up to the plate.

Because Drevin is *good*. Suddenly, the Paddle Creek Panthers were winning not just games but championships, and gay players were coming from all over the country to play for the town. There's a lot of boarded-up real estate around here, but the businesses that are open are more often than not run by people from the LGBT-plus community. Even the local biker gang is a rainbow-centric chapter, encouraging more and more like-minded people here.

Hence giving the town such a high quality of life score when it comes to being queer. When I moved out of my parents' house, my only concern was to get as far away as possible. Paddle Creek looked both welcoming and cheap, so I packed my bags and never looked back.

As I dance in the living room with my friends to an old Shakira song, I grin over the lip of my Solo cup and let my gaze travel across the room. I might be a cynical mother-fucker, but even I can admit that I've grown fond of this place and the (sometimes slightly odd) people who live here. I'm glad I've got myself a small apartment lined up to live with another friend and an entry-level office job to pay for it. I'm sure I'll be bored out of my skull, but it'll be worth it to know that I'm safe and welcomed everywhere I go.

Almost everywhere.

"Warning," Harper grumbles, glaring over my shoulder. "Trouble at twelve o'clock."

Jessie and I turn our heads to see what he's talking about. Jessie grunts in exasperation and rolls his eyes. Whereas my heart does that weird flip-flop thing it always does when I see Logan McKenna out in the wild.

The problem with incredibly good-looking closeted guys is that they're like god-damned catnip to me. No strings attached, and all that pent-up frustration? Sign me the fuck up.

It took little to no time at all to lure him into bed, and the secret sex has been addictive. There was never any chance of catching feels because—quite frankly—he's a dick. Not just to other people, but to himself. Internalized homophobia is toxic, and I'm not interested in being around that any longer than it takes to come my brains out.

And that's fine. I swore I'd never let anyone else get close to my heart and I mean it. The one person I trusted with it left it slashed in tatters. No one's ever going to hurt me like that again.

So I don't care that Logan has his girlfriend hanging on his arm. I'd feel sorry for her, but Tara Sherman is just plain mean and deserves a little karma coming her way. I'm not jealous of her, though. I don't wish I was the one dating Logan McKenna.

But try as I might, I'm not some hollow, emotionless creature. I've let that man inside my body on numerous occasions, and yet when our paths cross in public, he makes a point of sneering at me. Even laughing at me. If there's one person I'd be keen to avoid now that I've graduated, it'll be him. I told him as much the last time we hooked up.

It's over. He wasn't happy.

He told me I was being a pussy and that he liked fucking me because he didn't have to do that 'girl shit' with me. The deal was that I wasn't supposed to care or have feelings, that it was just about sex, and I agreed. But him treating me like garbage out in the real world crosses a line.

It also comes perilously close to echoing the words my Daddy told me when he ended our relationship the summer before. The ones that cut me to the bone and left me a broken wreck of a boy.

Look, I love my kink. Being a lifeless doll and letting a guy have his way with me is exhilarating. It lets me get out of my head and just be someone else's beautiful prop. But I didn't claw my way out of that suffocating, conservative hell hole where I grew up only to be told that my opinions don't matter. That I'm still someone who should be seen and not heard.

Logan doesn't get to decide when I matter or not. I do. I don't want to be his boyfriend, but I'm not going to let him dehumanize me out in the real world, either.

So my breath hitches as he and Tara enter the room. I only have a second to wonder how he's going to react, then the problem is solved for me. In a matter of speaking.

"What are you doing here, traitor?" Tara sneers at Jessie, who crosses his arms and narrows his eyes at her.

"It's a free country," Jessie says defiantly. "If anything, I should be asking what *you're* doing here. You decided to fuck around and find out, so you're not on the squad anymore. This is a Panthers house. I'm here with the Kittens. You know? The team you quit."

Tara looks my friend up and down with a curled lip. "Whatever, freak. I'd rather quit than be associated with a drug-dealing biker gang and that crazy old cat man who you let fuck you."

Jessie looks murderous and steps forward, but I put my hand protectively on his chest and laugh. "She's not worth it, hon."

And that's when this blonde bitch turns her attention to me. *"You,"* she rasps. "Another little freak that deserves to be locked up."

I scoff. "Oh, sweetheart, threatening me with handcuffs isn't going to get you the reaction you're hoping for."

She makes a repulsed face and moves closer to Logan, who automatically wraps his arm around her waist. "Fancy seeing you here, Hughes," he says smoothly. I grit my teeth and force my dick not to jump like Pavlov's fucking dog at the sound of his voice. Damn, that boy loved dirty talk and at the time, it was fun.

I'm not interested in hearing another word from him if he can't at least treat me with a modicum of civility.

"McKenna," I say curtly. "We were here first, so either deal with it or find somewhere else to spend your Friday night. I hear Clayton, the school raccoon, is hosting a rave behind the dumpsters."

I flash a grin at him as several people laugh. Even over the music, our little interaction is earning some attention. It's not surprising, really. Logan's kind of the closest thing this town has to a celebrity or royal family. His dad is mega-rich and owns half the public property around here. The rumor is that he's waiting until he has enough to flatten it all and start from scratch, gentrifying the whole area. He even used to own the football team, and they almost renamed the stadium after him.

I never did ask Logan why that fell through. Probably because I don't care. I bet his dad is just as awful as he is. I never met him officially, just saw him once from afar. God damn it, why does Logan have to be so pretty?

Neither Logan nor Tara likes being laughed at. "Can it, Hughes," Tara snaps at me. "Your blatant crush on my boyfriend is so pathetic. Give it up. He'd never fuck you in a million years."

I blink at her and laugh. "Is that so?" I say, flicking my gaze toward Logan, who's gone stiff as a board. "And what makes you think I'd ever fuck *him* in a million years?"

She rolls her eyes. "He told me all about how you begged him so many times. See, we don't keep secrets in this relationship."

This is becoming less funny. I try not to give a shit what others think of me. But I *hate* people lying about me. Yeah, okay, I slept with her boyfriend, which is not a great look. However, *he* pursued *me. He's* the one who insists on publicly dating a girl, even though he's as gay as RuPaul in West Hollywood at Pride. It's not a real relationship and she's awful, so personally I don't consider it cheating. Not when I specifically only wanted him for his body and not his poisonous personality.

I knew this would come back to bite me in the ass. Great sex isn't worth getting tangled up in their drama and lies.

"I seem to remember the begging was the other way around," I say coolly to Logan.

For a fraction of a second, his eyes go wide. Then he barks out a laugh. "In your dreams, Hughes. I'm not a fucking fag, and even if I were, I'd never degrade myself with a nobody like you."

"Good thing you don't have to anymore," I retort. "It's over, remember? Why don't you admit to yourself and your clueless girlfriend that you're just as much of a fag as I am?"

"If anyone's clueless, it's you," he snarls, hugging Tara to his side. "Be as deluded as you want, but don't drag my girl into it. She's everything you're not."

"I *know*. She has a *vagina*," I say in exasperation, throwing out my hands.

People are laughing again, but Logan grits his teeth and leans closer to me. "She's rich, beautiful, and smart. You should shut your mouth and leave us alone, you freak."

He releases Tara and gets in my face, his blazing eyes locked with mine. I jut my chin up defiantly. We're about the same height, so I'm not going to let him intimidate me.

Or at least I'll try. When he speaks, it's so low only I can hear him.

"Don't fucking test me, princess," he snarls. "I know you better than you think. You're so desperate for someone to tell you that you matter, but you don't. You say you don't do feelings, but that's only because deep down, you know you're unlovable. Your fancy family didn't want you, and neither did your ex-boyfriend. We had something good, and if you think breaking it off is going to make me respect you, then you are tragically misinformed. You're *nothing*, and you'll always be *nothing*."

I step back, my heart racing.

Suddenly, I'm not at the party anymore. I'm back in Daddy Stanley's bedroom as he packs my things and tells me he's bored of me.

"If I wanted someone else's opinion, I'd date a real man. You're supposed to be my doll, and you can't even do that right."

I'd never been so degraded in my life. I'd felt utterly

worthless. At least I knew my parents never really loved me, and it was a relief to escape them. With Stanley, it was supposed to be different. But in the end, he made me feel even worse than they ever did. Like it was mortifying that I ever thought I had opinions that mattered or that my voice should be heard. I've never cried so hard before or since that night.

It takes me a horrifying second to realize that tears are sliding down my face in the here and now.

"Oh my god!" Tara cries gleefully at Logan. "He's so obsessed with you that you made him blub!" She glares at me again. "So pathetic. Get it through your empty head, freak! He's never going to fuck you, ever!"

This can't be happening. No, no, *no!* I worked so hard to make sure I was never vulnerable in front of anyone in my new life so they wouldn't have the ammunition to hurt me like Stanley did or like my parents tried to do. I've spent the last year in control, and Logan McKenna is undoing all of that in a matter of minutes. People are still looking at us, but they aren't laughing anymore.

Their expressions are ones of pity.

"Okay, that's enough," Harper shouts as Jessie wraps his arms around me. But it's like a dam has broken and every emotion I've done my best to lock away over the past several years is tumbling out now.

I'm not sure what's worse. Tara's lies or Logan's truth.

I *hate* that he has the measure of me like that. I do put on a front and pretend like no one can get close enough to touch me because that's the way I want it. The reality is that I'm so terrified that if someone breaks me down like that again, I won't recover. My parents treated me like nothing, only for Stanley to confirm it was true.

I swore I'd never feel that way again.

"Fuck you," I snarl through gritted teeth, jabbing a finger

into Logan's face as tears drip from my chin. "You weren't worth it. I wish you a miserable, closeted life. I'll be out here loud and proud, living my truth. *You're* the one who's pathetic."

Logan laughs at me. "This is my town, Hughes, and there's not a damn thing you can do about it."

I guess people like him really don't get kink. He doesn't understand that because I used to let him take charge in the bedroom, it doesn't mean I'm helpless in the real world. I never even dressed up for him or went full doll mode. He'd have lost his mind, and not in a good way. But he thinks because I was a pillow princess for him in bed that he gets to dictate how I live my life now?

Nuh-uh.

"Oh, we'll see about that," I say with a savage grin. It's my turn to speak so quietly we're the only two who can hear me. "You want to tarnish my reputation? I'll destroy yours, pretty boy. Just you wait."

He laughs again, but this time it's uncertain, and he frowns at me. In that moment, I wish I had some proof as to just how much of a fake he is, but I don't.

Between his vicious words and the way he made me lose it in front of everyone, I'm afraid to admit I'm pretty devastated. I put up all these walls to keep myself safe. But breaking off our arrangement obviously hurt him more than he'd care to admit. He went for my metaphorical jugular and left me bleeding out on the floor with everyone else standing around, watching. Sure, my friends tried to support me, but I never wanted them to see me like that, either.

Paddle Creek has been my do-over. My clean slate. Even after Stanley, I refused to move. This is my home. Am I going to have to run from here as well?

I look between Jessie and Harper, who are still clinging to me, and Logan and Tara as they laugh at me. The crowd looks awkward, and the music feels uncomfortably loud. Oh, *fuck.*

Some people have their phones out. They've got one of the worst moments of my life on camera for all the world to see.

I wish I'd filmed Logan. I'd smear his name so fast his head would spin. He wants to make me out to be something I'm not? The truth would be far more damning for him. All his very loud homophobia would come back to bite him in the ass.

But I don't have a single shred of evidence.

Not yet, anyway.

I can be patient. No one gets to make me feel like this. No one has that kind of power over me, at least not for long. I swore I'd never let anyone treat me like my parents or Stanley did ever again, and I mean it.

"Hey, what's going on?"

A nerdy-looking guy in glasses pushes his way through the crowd. It's Gabriel Visoth, a sophomore I'm friends with and I think the only non-football player who's a member of Alpha Zeta Kappa. He's closer to Jessie than to me, but I do know that his two ex-Panther boyfriends are also his Daddies. Despite being a small geek, he's got a lot of respect around here.

People look sheepish, and I'm glad for an excuse to snap out of this ordeal. I've had quite enough humiliation for one evening. Besides, the way Gabe is glaring at Logan, he's not thrilled to see him either. I feel like I can walk away with some dignity intact. Time to make a swift exit.

"This isn't over," I snarl at Logan.

He huffs and rolls his eyes. "Yeah, sure, Hughes. I'm quaking in my boots."

For a second, I hold his gaze, long enough for him to swallow nervously.

Gotcha. I mean it. He's going to rue the day he ever fucked with me.

With one last disdainful flick of my eyes up and down the body I used to worship, I shake off my friends and storm toward the front door. I'm not in the mood to party anymore.

I've got revenge to plan.

CHAPTER 2

Rafferty

The atmosphere in the back of the limo is tense. I can usually muster up the energy to play nice when it's for a charity event, but it's becoming increasingly more difficult to toe the line when I'm faced with such barely concealed contempt.

My wife and I do not love each other. I'm not certain we ever loved each other. For a time, when we were first married in a match that was beneficial to both our families and their businesses, we had common goals. Seeing as we are both undeniably hard workers, we strove toward those goals together, and for a few years, it felt like contentment.

I find happiness in success. No one who truly knows us would ever dare to call our marriage a success now, unless they are referring to how well we manage to deceive the public and the tabloids.

I wish it didn't matter. Why do they care? I've begged Charleen for a divorce more times than I can count, but she says that it would destroy everything we've built over the past twenty-five years. My argument that if it can be ruined that easily then maybe it wasn't that strong to begin with has been steadfastly ignored.

So I put up with it. I barely have to see her unless there are cameras present or if our son, Logan, is going to be around. I'm sure we're not fooling him, but that's what we do in this family. We lie.

I know he's gay and refuses to come out, no doubt thanks to his mother and her rotten parents. They're the kind of people who aren't openly prejudiced but I have no doubt it's left Logan with the distinct impression he'd be quietly disowned if he ever confessed to his sexuality publicly. It makes me sick, and it's certainly twisted him into a young man I barely recognize anymore.

Charleen spends most of her time in California with her younger architect lover. I suspect she always wanted to be with someone a great deal more malleable than I am. She likes to take charge, but so do I. For the life of me, I don't understand why we don't just end this sham marriage so she can go off into the sunset with her pretty little boy toy.

As for me, I don't have the strength to even consider a relationship. My business is my priority, and the thought of juggling a secret affair on top of managing my family just makes me feel exhausted. Discrete trysts and occasional filthy private parties generally see that my needs get met. There's usually a pretty little treat looking for a sugar Daddy to pamper her, even if it's only for a night.

Lies, lies, lies. That's all the McKennas have. I'm sick of it. This evening has been increasingly grating after Charleen made us later and later for the benefit dinner, then spent the whole drive bitching at me like it was somehow my fault.

She's not a bad person. Not really. It's just sometimes people aren't meant to be together. They actively bring out the worst in each other simply by standing next to one another.

I don't think I can do this anymore.

Charleen blinks at me, and I feel a shift in the air between us.

"I beg your pardon?"

Shit. I said that out loud, didn't I?

I sigh and look at her. She is stunning. Age has only made her more refined, more powerful. I can understand why that puppy of an architect is besotted with her. But as we sit in the back of the limo, I see clearer than ever that we're simply two magnets pointing the wrong way at each other.

"Nothing. We're nearly there," I say, jutting my chin to indicate the tall hotel we're approaching.

Usually, I spend my time between our home in Albertson and the nearby towns where a lot of my business is wrapped up. Including Paddle Creek—a foolish investment that I've been wasting my time on for more than fifteen years. Sunk cost fallacy dictates I should sell up and walk away. But I've been trying my best to remodel that town for so long, and I'm a stubborn mule when I want to be. I'm holding out until I can get my way. It's not like my other developments are suffering from it.

But sometimes I do get too obsessed, so it's good to get away into the city every now and again. The fundraiser is on the northern outskirts of Indianapolis, and I'm sure it will do us both good to mingle with society for an evening.

"I'm not having this conversation with you again, Rafferty," Charleen snips.

"Neither am I," I observe.

We are genuinely pulling up the drive to the hotel now and there's nothing else I feel like adding. But I know she needs to get her opinion across whether I like it or not, so I resign myself to getting an earful.

"We're not children. Nor are we trailer trash. We present a united, successful front so that confidence in us does not waver from our peers, investors, colleagues, or even acquaintances. We *are* this company. If you've got a slip of a thing desperate for a big society wedding, tell her now that it's never going to happen. The McKenna family name always has and always will come first."

I fight the urge to point out that it's *my* family name, not hers. The Doboshes are equally respectable, but not as flashy as my lot. The McKennas have a better origin story, having come over from Ireland a hundred years ago and growing our fortunes generation by generation.

Besides, she just likes having my balls in a vise.

Sighing, I turn to look at her. The limo has stopped, and the doorman has opened her door. "There isn't any slip of a thing," I assure her truthfully. "I'm just tired."

"Then take some pharmaceuticals like a normal person and stop bitching," she says coolly before exiting the car.

I take a second to scrub my hand over my clean-shaven chin before pulling myself together and exiting from my own door, which has also been opened for me. If the staff think anything of our brief pause, they don't give any indication of it. Just another lie to cover up in the life of the McKennas.

No matter what Charleen is truly feeling in that moment, she won't let it show. So I walk around the limo to find her waiting to take my arm. She puts on a dazzling smile as we walk through the front entrance. "Come on, darling," she says amicably. "There's nothing to quarrel about. Let's go have a nice evening, hmm?"

I muster a small smile and a nod to appease her, knowing that's much easier for her to say than it is for me to do. Socializing and networking come so naturally to her. It's like a drug that feeds her. Whereas I can happily chat for hours with people I know well on subjects that interest me. However, small talk bores me to tears.

Just a few hours, I promise myself. That's all I have to do.

The hotel's ballroom is already brimming with people milling around in dresses and tuxes. Chandeliers glitter overhead, and a string quartet plays in the corner, their gentle music drifting over the polite conversation.

A savage part of me thinks that every single person in this room is just like us—hiding dirty secrets behind simpering smiles. It's all so painfully fake. Even the event itself is a shame. Supposedly, it's fundraising for a charity that helps battered women and children, which I agree is a noble cause. But none of those people are here tonight, save for a couple that are being paraded around in clothes that have no doubt been loaned to them. This evening is more about the rich patting themselves on the back for what a nice thing they're doing. It's about making sure you've been seen doing a good deed.

I doubt many of these people would be involved if it were simply anonymous donations.

Sighing, I take two Champagne flutes from a passing server's tray, and hand one to Charleen as she gravitates toward a cluster of women that I assume she knows. I'm wallowing in bitterness because I'm feeling out of control, so instead, I'm lashing out. I'm fully aware that this is how business gets done. An event like this will raise ten times what a simple donation drive would do.

But there's an itch within me that's desperate to be scratched. Is it too much to ask for a real fucking human interaction without all this bullshit getting in the way? It doesn't have to be pretty. Right now, I just need something authentic.

For the next couple of hours, however, I play nice. As far as any of these people are concerned, I am a dutiful husband who is riveted by the conversation over dinner. I bid a ridiculous amount on several items, most of which I don't want, but I console myself that the cause is actually a worthy one. I'm sure I can find places to put the modern art, and Charleen will happily take the gifted experiences off my hands.

After dessert has been served and people are once again wandering around the room to mingle, I feel like I've done my duty and suffered enough. If I don't get this tie off in the next five minutes, I'm going to suffocate.

I manage to catch Charleen between conversations and lean in to whisper against her ear. "I'm going to order a ride. You take the limo home. If anyone asks, you can tell them I have a headache." They won't ask, but she'll like to think they will.

She's either going to pitch a fit or not care. Apparently, she's had a good night because she waves me off with her hand. "Go. Have fun," she murmurs, already drifting away to another group of friends with a "Darling! It's been too long!"

I don't need her permission, but it makes life easier with her approval.

My phone is already in my hand before I've even made it through the doors. I hadn't really thought past getting the hell out of there, possibly seeking company, possibly searching for solitude. I've had a few drinks, so I could either continue drowning my sorrows or sober up pretty quickly. My app shows several executive cars within five minutes of the hotel. I just need to decide on a destination.

That's when I see the notification that's popped up on my calendar. 'Drinks with the Joneses.' The discrete code I use for a kink event. My heart flips. Good god, that's exactly what I need right now. People who aren't afraid to ask for what they really want and just fucking take it. The calendar reminder doesn't give me any further details, so I pause in the foyer and sift through my emails to work out which event in particular this is.

Oh, fantastic. It's a private residential event being hosted literally on the way back between here and home. I know the organizers. They're stringent about screening their guests and not allowing cellphones, so I always feel safe going to their meetups. There's a strong chance there will be people there I've already played with. A familiar, easy scene or just some quick and dirty orgasms sound incredible in this moment.

It's like there was a rubber band around my chest that I didn't even realize was there until it started loosening. I hastily punch the address into my ride app, then go to wait outside in the fresh night air.

I know that I bitch a lot about the constraints of my life, but I'm also fully aware that I have an enormous amount of privilege. Looking up at what few stars I can see through the light pollution, I feel free again. Even if it's only for a night. For the next few hours, I can actually be authentic. I might never see these people I'm about to meet again, but that doesn't mean we can't share something real and meaningful. Hopefully, that will give me the fortitude to bullshit my way through the next several weeks until I can let loose again.

It'll have to. I'm not escaping the façade of my marriage anytime soon. Tonight will top up my reservoir and give me the strength to keep up the lies and bullshit life requires of me.

So I better cherish this time and not waste it.

CHAPTER 3

Kadence

I KNOW MY FRIENDS ARE WORRIED ABOUT ME. IF I'M BEING honest, I'm worried about me, too.

Logan McKenna broke something in me that night. Something fragile that I've clung to throughout all the bullshit with my family. Since Stanley unceremoniously dumped me.

The timing is spectacularly bad as well, that's easy enough to see. Now that I'm done with college, I no longer have an aim or a purpose. I envy people like my friend Harper, who so clearly has a career goal in mind. I've started this menial office job, and my only motivation is the paycheck, so I don't starve or get kicked out of my new apartment.

As I drive along the interstate, I smile ruefully to myself in the dark. My apartment has an additional perk in the form of Erika, my friend and now housemate. She's the reason I dragged my sorry ass out of bed, found some clothes and makeup, and eventually hauled myself on the road in the direction of this party.

Erika is a pretty dyke a couple of years older than me who I met on the scene a little while ago. Our mutual disdain for bullshit drew us together, and when her former house-mate moved out, she offered me the room first. I jumped at the chance, knowing it would be much easier to live with someone who was already well aware of the side of myself I keep hidden even from my friends.

She's recently become a Dommy to a newly divorced woman in her late thirties who's trying out being a little—not to mention a relationship with a woman—for the first time. It's all incredibly adorable, but much like with my other friends, nothing I want to play third wheel to. I mentioned this party to Erika sometime last week, so she knew full well what she was doing when she announced that they were having a playdate at the apartment tonight and that I needed to make myself scarce.

Stupid friend making me leave my stupid home for my stupid mental health.

Yeah, okay. Maybe there have been a few days since The Incident when I didn't feel like showering. And maybe I've been late to work most days, but I was still *there*, so I'm not sure what the big deal is. And, okay, maybe living off ramen noodles and cherry cola was making my tummy hurt.

Maybe…just *maybe*…I needed some help to snap myself out of that shit.

But it's as if Logan and Tara found my Achilles heel and not only slashed it, but they laid my mangled body out for everyone to laugh at. Every time I think about all those people seeing me crying and shaking, it's like I'm back in that moment all over again, belly exposed and begging for mercy that doesn't come.

It still doesn't make sense to me. I feel like I've had bigger traumatic events than that in my life. But something about Logan's words, in particular, has just left me feeling so completely out of control that I figuratively curled up into a fetal position and haven't left it since.

Until now.

Knowing I had no choice but to leave the apartment and having this party dangled in front of me, it forced me into the shower where the pettiness grew as if fueled by the hot water blasting against my skin. Why should I be the one cowering? I am phenomenal. I am independent. I am going to this kink event and have any man I want wrapped around my finger.

As I had all day to get ready, I luxuriated in pampering every inch of my body. Luckily, I'm up to date with all my waxing, but I had a proper shave of my face complete with a hot towel treatment first thing in the morning to give my pores time to recover. I then took the time to scrub and moisturize my skin until it glowed before styling my permed curls to perfection. Sometimes I think about growing my hair long enough that I could play with extensions when I feel like it. But I like the juxtaposition of my shorter cut with my hyper feminine doll looks. It makes me feel powerful.

That's what I need tonight.

My manicure is still fine from my last appointment, so I spend the evening focusing on my makeup. Contrary to what a lot of men might assume, just because it's not a drag look doesn't mean I don't take just as long to appear this naturally flawless. When I'm being fucked senseless later, I don't want a single smudge on this beat mug.

The best thing about house parties is that I can drive right up to the front door, so there's almost no worry about getting exposed in public with what I'm wearing. It's not that I'm ever ashamed or think that I don't look stunning. It's more that other people are ignorant jackasses, and I have no interest in getting a beating.

Pain isn't my kink.

So I might have sensible shoes on right now to make managing the pedals easier, and I'm also wrapped up in a long coat. But underneath is pure sin, and once I get through that front door, nothing is going to hold me back.

I deserve this. I'm a good person. Okay, I'm not a *bad* person, not really. I'm owed a little fun for the shit sandwich the universe dealt me last week. Once I've got my head screwed back on, I can stop moping around, and my friends will no longer be calling me every hour to make sure I haven't done anything drastic.

As soon as I'm myself again, I can start working on how I'm going to make Logan McKenna feel as horrendous as I did. The universe will then be back in balance, and I can get on with the rest of my life.

And that all starts tonight.

I am going to go to this party and be so unapologetically myself that it rattles me back to my senses. I can't let some fuck boi strip me of my identity, especially one I'm not even fucking anymore. It was only ever a casual thing between us, and if Logan couldn't cope with me ending it, that's his deal. Perhaps if he came out of the closet, he might be a bit less tense all the damn time.

I am fully aware that I'm a walking contradiction. It was supposed to be casual and no strings attached, but him ignoring me—or worse, sneering at me—was dehumanizing. I didn't want him to put a ring on it, but that didn't mean I wasn't looking for a little respect. I only wanted to be dehumanized on *my* terms.

Laughing ruefully, I take the turn my app tells me to. My friend Jessie is a kitten, and I can understand that mentality quite well. I'm like a cat that wants to be let outside only to immediately turn around and complain that it's too cold and I want back in.

That's just who I am. I doubt I'll ever find anyone to put up with my contrariness long term, as Stanley so cruelly pointed out to me. But it's not like I'm even looking for that.

Especially not tonight. No. Tonight, I just want to escape my own head and have some hot guy fuck my brains out. Is that too much to ask?

I've been to parties at this place before. I like the couple that both run the events and own the mansion that I'm pulling up to. They're in their fifties and don't take part in the sex themselves. I think they get off on watching their guests a lot, but there's also a sweet side to them that tells me that they genuinely enjoy facilitating people getting together.

I find a space to park where I hopefully won't be blocked in later when I want to leave, then kill the ignition and take a deep breath. Still inside my car and away from the house, it's nice and quiet. I'm not sure I could ever live in the countryside, but I do appreciate the tranquility of a place like this.

Not to mention it makes having big orgies a lot easier when there aren't any nosy neighbors around.

As I exit my car, the late spring air has a slight chill to it, but not enough to deter me from changing out here so I can make a proper grand entrance at the front door. I don't want to be holding a coat and looking for a cloakroom. I want to sweep in there like the belle of the ball that I am.

So I swap my sensible woolen outer layer for a gauzy black robe with a feathered collar and cuffs and kick off my sneakers to trade for a pair of satin pumps. On my body I'm wearing baby doll lingerie, specifically designed with a flat bralette for people who don't have boobs. The skirt skims my thighs, and the black gauze has colorful flowers embroidered all over it. My lacy jockstrap hugs my cock and leaves very little to the imagination, not to mention gives extremely easy access to my hole.

People could accuse me of being many things, but subtle isn't one of them.

As I walk confidently toward the house, gliding over the gravel like a pro in my heels, a small, fluffy black purse swings from my wrist. It contains my car keys, lube, condoms, lipstick, and gloss.

Everything a girl could possibly want.

The drive has spotlights to illuminate the way, and the house itself has warm light glowing from every window. I see several shapes moving behind the blinds, giving me a glimpse of what's about to come. My heart beats faster, but it's a good kind of adrenaline.

It might seem strange to some people, but I feel at home in places like this. I'm slightly nervous because I want to have a good time, especially after the atrocious week I've had. But I'm not afraid of rejection or humiliation here. It's more like anxious anticipation of who I'm going to meet and what might happen rather than feeling worried about being exposed and then getting hurt while I'm vulnerable.

One of the husbands, Jason, opens the door and immediately looks me up and down with hungry eyes. "Well, aren't you just the tastiest treat?" he purrs as he ushers me inside.

"I like to think so," I agree, fluttering my eyelashes. "Are there any Daddies here tonight you think might gobble me up?"

Jason snorts. "Plenty," he says with a wink.

Good. I've had it with scared little boys. Time to find myself a real man for a night of fun.

One of the distinguishing features of Jason and Markus's parties is that they're for everyone. That's a double win for me. I hate going to 'male-only' spaces and then getting treated like shit for being too fem. Equally, parties like tonight's keep away the kind of 'gold star' gays who want to toss their cookies at the mere hint of a vagina or some boobies.

It not only makes the events trans inclusive but also accepting of people of any orientation, even straight people. All kinksters are welcome under this roof. I'll be honest, I'm almost always looking for a more masculine energy to dominate me, but I know there are those who get confused by my vibe.

There are those who think someone this pretty shouldn't have a big, juicy cock. They would be wrong.

As usual, there's a table in the entrance foyer with several glass bowls. Each has different colored rubber bangles inside, although some of them are looking a little diminished. Good. That means lots of people are already here. I wanted to be fashionably late. No point putting this much effort into an outfit if I can't parade through the house and show it off before I start getting ravaged.

The colors each mean something different, like that you're looking for a specific gender to play with or you're open to anything. That you're a Dom, sub, top, bottom, or again, open to anything. Water sports, bondage, pain play. There's even one if you're not here for sex but perhaps some age play or humiliation, or perhaps you just want to be petted and told you're pretty.

Looking at all the labeled options makes me smile as I think of all the people here tonight feeling free and living their best lives. It makes me proud to be alive in a time and place where we're able to express ourselves like this without fear of getting arrested or worse. It really wasn't that long ago when queer people had no rights at all, and there are plenty of places on this planet—hell, in this country—where it's still dangerous.

Rather than ponder on that sad truth, I select a few bangles and head straight to the kitchen for a refreshment. I'm not drinking alcohol as I want to drive home and, besides, the highs I'm planning to chase will be intoxicating enough. But I do want to stay hydrated for all the wild sex I'm hoping I'll be having shortly, so I fetch myself a cup of the fruit punch and take a handful of grapes.

I had food before I left the apartment, but I find grapes are perfect for encouraging people to look at my glossy mouth as well as helping keep up my fluid levels. Not to mention making me feel like a cherub from ancient Greece on his way to partake in some debauchery with the god of wine and ecstasy, Dionysus. I smile to myself, secretly thanking Professor Knight for my classics education, which I'm obviously putting to very good use.

The kitchen is off-limits for sexy times for hygiene reasons, but as soon as I start wandering through the rest of the enormous mansion, I'm quickly surrounded by people in various stages of undress, passion, and wickedness.

It's magnificent.

My cock thickens right away as I watch a veritable feast of fucking. People lying back in seats as they receive oral. Group activities. Bondage and discipline displays. Sweat dripping from skin and moans slipping from throats. The air is thick with sounds and smells, and it feels so *alive* to me.

Not everyone is taking part. Plenty are watching, either resting between fun times themselves or taking in the sights like the hosts themselves. There are no rules against drinking, although there are volunteers helping Jason and Markus keeping an eye on everyone to make sure nothing unsafe happens. One of the downstairs rooms houses the main bar, where there are more people relaxing in the shadows than engaging in activities. That's not to say there isn't *anything* delicious happening in here. It's just a little more chilled.

It's a perfect place for me to take a turn about the room like a real Jane Austen heroine and survey the scene, scouting for potential playdates. My gaze is immediately drawn to an older gentleman in what my gut tells me to be an extremely expensive suit. Out of the corner of my eye, I spot him walking across the room, and I look over my shoulder just in time to see him take a free seat in a plush armchair, sipping on a crystal tumbler of an amber liquid I assume to be whiskey.

He seems like the kind of man to drink whiskey. I can't say I like the stuff, but I know I want to taste it on his lips.

Then I study his face a moment longer, and my heart more or less stops altogether.

I know this man.

And not as in I've seen him around parties like this before or even met him in real life. As in I've seen his photo in news articles. As in he was at that protest outside the former mayor's house last summer.

As in he's Logan's dad.

My initial knee-jerk reaction is to flee. The idea of anything to do with Logan being here in my safe space makes me panic. But before I can take more than three steps, I stop myself, frowning and moving into a more secluded corner of the room.

Why does this feel important? What's stopping me from getting the hell out of here?

Because Logan's father is extremely wealthy and famous. If it came out that he's going to parties like this and he's into kinky shit, surely that would cause a scandal, right?

The kind of scandal that might ruin a man…his family… his son…

Am I seriously considering this? In all my hours of moping over the past week, I've been so fixated on how it would feel to get the revenge I promised against Logan. But in my mind, I always skipped past the pesky 'how' part. Could it really be this easy? Do opportunities like this actually fall into people's laps?

Apparently so.

Okay, if I go ahead with this crazy idea and throw myself at this man—who to all intents and purposes I believe to be straight—will he even be interested in me? And how would I prove anything actually happened? There are no cameras of any kind allowed in here for precisely that reason.

So I need to prove he's a deviant *outside* of the party.

My heart is still banging in my chest, but for different reasons now. I'm excited. I move in the shadows, stalking my prey from afar. I can see where Logan gets his good looks from. If anything, Daddy McKenna is even hotter. A real silver fox. It's a little difficult to tell through the suit what his body's like, but he's no couch potato, that's for sure. His salt-and-pepper hair is thick and just the right length for pulling on. He's got a strong, clean-shaven jaw and sparkling eyes and…yep. If I'm seriously thinking about seducing him, the physical attraction won't be a problem.

At least for me. I can't see his bangles with the way his suit jacket is currently sitting. He might not be into men. In fact, I know for a fact he's married to a woman. Does that mean anything, though? Countless powerful men throughout history have married conventionally so they'll be accepted by society and then spent their lives fucking men in secret.

Is that why Daddy McKenna is here?

I force myself to take a deep breath, then drink my punch and discard what's left of the grapes along with the cup into a trash can. Re-applying my lip gloss, I think if this is really what I want to do. I'm talking about getting compromising photos of a man who technically hasn't done anything wrong to me.

But he's sure raised a rotten son. Logan *hurt* me. Worse than that—he almost broke me entirely. He's morally bankrupt. If that's anyone's fault, it's got to be this man's as Logan's parent, right? Logan is a cruel bully, and I can't let him get away with this.

Do I care about my own reputation? I could destroy my future prospects as well if I splash myself all over the internet.

Not if I blur out my face. Or turn my back to the camera. Or stay out of the photos altogether. Maybe all I need is to truss up Daddy McKenna in a fun outfit, stuff something ridiculous up his ass, then video what comes next.

Now *that* would be powerful.

Logan's family name would be disgraced. He thinks he's untouchable, but no one is. Not if you're vindictive enough. Besides, men like his father don't get that rich without fucking other people over. I'm sure this guy has it coming to him and then some.

In fact, if I bring him down a peg or two, it'll practically be a *noble* cause. I'm sure I'll be doing plenty of people a favor. Maybe even his wife. Does she know he's here?

Probably not. Like father, like son. I think of Tara laughing at me and how she had no idea just how many times my pretty, tight hole had made her boyfriend come his brains out.

At that moment, Daddy McKenna's gaze flicks my way. Even in the darkness, it seems he could tell he was being watched. Our eyes meet.

I guess this is it. Now or never. Decision time.

Revenge? Or live and let live?

Ultimately, it's not even a hard choice to make.

This is going to be *fun.*

CHAPTER 4

Rafferty

I'M BEING WATCHED.

The prickling sensation is actually quite stimulating. After my wife ignored me all evening, I love the idea that I've caught the attention of a pretty girl. I deliberately don't look directly, giving her time to approach me. But I can make out long, creamy legs, the swish of black fabric, and the glow of a beautifully made-up face.

So I spend the next couple of minutes sipping my whiskey, feeling the buzz thrumming through my veins, and enjoying watching the blonde with bouncy tits getting sensually but thoroughly spit-roasted by two guys who keep grinning and kissing each other.

Every few minutes, the relief of how pleased I am to have made the decision to come here washes over me. I'm so incredibly happy not to be at the awful, fake party anymore. So far, I've only delighted in observing others. But if this gorgeous creature comes any closer to me, I'm probably in with an excellent chance of getting my cock sucked in no time at all.

I think that's what I want right now. For someone to

make me feel good and not have to worry about their needs. I know that's selfish, but if I'm honest and upfront, where's the harm, really? I'm not here to pretend. I'm not here to make friends.

I'm here to feel free.

Finally, I sense my stalker approaching, moving slowly but confidently out of the shadows. I flick my eyes toward her...and pause.

The face sure is stunning, and I was right about the floaty, gauzy material. It's both a robe and a floral dress. But through it, I can clearly see a flat chest and a barely concealed cock nestled in lacy underwear.

Huh.

Not what I was expecting, but I find myself holding their gaze as they come closer. They really are beautiful, and interest is still stirring down in my pants.

Maybe it's the high I'm feeling from being here rather than at the benefit dinner. Maybe it's curiosity. Maybe it's just the alcohol buzz. But I watch my new friend as they move in closer, eventually dropping their small purse to the floor, swishing their robe back, and sliding onto my lap. Their legs are draped across my thighs, one arm wrapping around my neck, and the other free hand resting on my chest, just above my heart.

"Hello, Daddy," they purr, licking glossy lips and looking at me through thick, dark eyelashes.

I do like being called Daddy.

"Hello, beautiful," I find myself replying. "Are you a good girl?"

"Hmm," they hum, tapping my chest with a manicured finger. "I'm a good doll. I have a boy pussy, and it's all ready and waiting for Daddy's hard cock."

Jesus. I was already turned on. It's hard not to be after all the people I've seen getting off tonight. But this little minx has got my length turning to steel in seconds.

So…a boy? A him. Normally, I wouldn't even consider the idea, but he really is gorgeous. Pretty eyes and pretty lips mere inches away from my face. Soft, smooth skin under my hand as I run my hand up his leg. And he smells divine, like candy with just a hint of spice.

Besides, it's not like I haven't experimented a couple of times back in the day. Who didn't at college? It's just human nature. It doesn't make me bisexual or any such nonsense. I'm absolutely straight. But…a hole's a hole at the end of the day.

This cutie says he's got one waiting for me.

"So, are you going to ride Daddy's lap?" I ask, feeling hopeful.

He giggles and bites his lip as he smiles down at me. "No, Daddy, Kiki's not like that."

I raise my eyebrows. "I take it you're Kiki?" He nods. "And does Kiki not want to play?"

He laughs again and shakes his head. "Oh, Kiki wants to play *very* much, Daddy. But Kiki is a doll. You play *with* me."

I frown, not quite following. "You're a pillow princess?" There goes my hope of a blow job with no reciprocation from me. But I have to admit…I probably won't mind putting in some effort for this beauty. He's enticing.

"I'm a doll, Daddy," Kiki says, leaning closer as he whispers to me. "A plaything. You get to do whatever you want to me, however you want. I'll be inanimate, yours to pose in whatever way you choose. I'll only talk if you want me to, and I only have a few phrases. Like a doll with a pull string. When we're together, my only purpose will be as a toy for you to use to make yourself feel *so fucking good.*"

He hisses the last part against the shell of my ear before nipping at the lobe.

Jesus Christ. My dick is actually painful right now, throbbing in my pants under the weight of his body. "Anything?"

He nods, looking at me through his long lashes. "Anything. You could make me face-fuck your cock right here or take me somewhere to bend me over and fill me with that big dick I can feel under my legs." He rolls his hips and presses down on my member, causing me to suck in a breath. He smirks, pleased with himself. "I've chosen you, Daddy. If you say yes, I'll go into doll mode, and you'll own me for however long you want."

My heart is racing. I usually like to dominate with my partners. It's another way in which Charleen and I are so incompatible as neither of us enjoys submitting. But what this beautiful boy is offering is another level of deliciousness.

"What if I want to watch you get fucked by someone else?" I ask.

He smiles and runs his thumb over my lower lip. "Of course, Daddy. Although I'd be a sad doll. It's your cock I want tonight."

He drops his hand back onto my chest. I mimic his gesture and rub my thumb against his lip as well. Except he takes it one step further and sucks the digit into his mouth, his burning gaze locked with mine.

"I've never played with a doll before," I tell him honestly. "But it sounds like a lot of fun, Kiki. Tell Daddy how it works. Can dolls walk, or do they need to be carried?"

He draws his head back, releasing my thumb before giving it a little kiss. "If you want to take me somewhere else, Daddy, I can walk if you tell me to. But if you want to carry me, I'd love that as well. Maybe the best way to explain is just to try it. If you want me to snap out of it, just safeword me."

He says it so calmly, his eyes smoldering and a little smile playing on his lips. But that takes me aback. I've never been in a situation where I've needed to safeword with a partner.

But other than using fluffy handcuffs a couple of times, I guess I haven't experimented much with kink. Not in a sexual limits way, I mean. I like being called Daddy and being in control of bedroom activities, that's for sure. I also like spoiling pretty young things if there's money to be spent. This is just the next logical step, I suppose.

"Okay," I say, almost like I'm negotiating a business deal. "And you can also safeword if necessary, yes?"

He nods, dragging his fingers in swirls over my sternum. "I doubt I'll need to. But yes. I can use a safeword if I need to. I just stick with red, yellow, and green. It's easiest. And if my mouth is full, I'll tap you twice if I need to stop."

It's pretty obvious he's done this before. I'm not used to feeling apprehensive when it comes to intimate situations, but I have to admit that I'm a tad out of my depth here. However, he explained it all pretty succinctly. I get to do whatever I want with him, and he'll be like a lifeless doll.

Is that going to feel a bit empty? Soulless? I search his eyes as he patiently watches me. He's offering to be *mine*. Completely. For me to have all the power over him. There's something exciting about that.

I have a lot of power in my life. But it's a long time since I actually felt *powerful*.

"Be a doll for me, Kiki," I murmur.

"Yes, Daddy," he rasps back.

His spine stiffens and he sits up straighter in my lap. At the same time, his facial expression becomes more neutral and his gaze slides to the middle distance. His hands relax with slightly curved fingers, his arms dropping so they're by his sides. I sense his core working to keep himself upright, so I wrap my arm around his waist to help steady him, taking a moment to marvel at his beauty.

"Can you say something else for me, pretty doll?"

"Please, Daddy," he says obediently, still looking ahead.

I run my free hand up his arm, across his chest, up his neck, and cup the side of his jaw. He doesn't move a muscle, allowing me to touch him however I want, just like he said.

Gently I turn his head so he's now facing me, and our eyes meet again. He doesn't blink.

I drag my fingers down his throat, feeling his slight Adam's apple, trailing my hand lower, over his stomach…

I pause at the top of his thigh, but he remains as still as a statue. So I take the opportunity to see if I have any interest in touching another man's cock. Back in my youth, I pretty much just let the other guy tend to himself while I took care of business from behind. But everything about Kiki is so pretty, it's drawing me in. I find myself wanting to explore.

Slipping my hand under the fluffy hem of the gauzy black dress, I skim my fingers over his warm skin until I find lace. He's not small and clearly aroused, which does my ego good. His immobility makes me feel emboldened. Like I'm free to experiment without the fear of fucking anything up. I know he's a stranger who I'm never going to see again, but my pride is telling me that I want this to be as good for him as it is for me. It's as if he's given me a gift by allowing me to play with him like this.

I don't want to disappoint him.

My palm strokes the full-feeling curve of his member under the lace. It's obviously different from what I'm used to, but I'm surprised to realize that the sentiment is the same. I want to touch him so he feels good.

"Do you like that, pretty doll?" I mumble against his lips. He still doesn't move, but I see the goose bumps on his skin and feel a rush of satisfaction.

"I love it, Daddy." His eyes are still locked on mine where I left him. I'm not even sure if he's blinked. I fondle his junk, almost daring him to react. But he doesn't, he just holds my gaze.

"Do you want more?" I ask, feeling my heart thumping in my chest.

"Yes, Daddy," he whispers. It's like he's punch drunk for me.

It turns out I love having my very own human doll to play with.

I see no reason to take this party elsewhere. Plus, I'm eager to see how Kiki responds to me moving him around. So I slip one arm under his knees and tighten my grip around his waist, leaning forward and encouraging him to stand. He does so, barely even swaying on the spot as I let him go.

He's mine. Mine, mine, *all mine.*

My pulse racing, I knock back the rest of my whiskey and place the glass down on a coaster that's resting on a small coffee table next to the armchair I'd been sitting in. Looking around, I find both a bowl of condoms and sachets of lube within reach. Jason and Markus always do take care of their guests well.

Knowing I'm all set to go, I just have to decide where I want my new-found toy.

Licking my lips, I look him up and down. He still hasn't moved, although he's just as beautiful as when I first laid eyes on him. I allow myself a second to pause and consider if this is something I'm genuinely interested in before I take the plunge. My cock is certainly hard, but am I attracted to this young man? Do I really want to take advantage of him in front of these people?

I trust them. No one here would ever betray me. Jason and Markus vet their guests thoroughly. But more than that, people here are generally aware of who I am. They know it wouldn't be worth their lives to fuck with me. Unlike back in that ballroom, here, I am invincible.

Besides, Kiki has given me very clear consent with the

added guarantee that either of us can back out anytime. The thing I can't deny no matter how much my head wants to puzzle it…is that I'm really attracted to him. I'm practically vibrating at the idea of getting my hands on him, of using him like he offered to make myself feel good.

I wanted authentic. He's just come and sat in my lap, called me Daddy, and begged me to fuck him. It doesn't get more transparent than that. He was open with his kink, and I really, *really* want to play. It doesn't matter that physically he's not quite what I'm used to.

Right now, all that matters is that he belongs to me.

With a sudden surge of energy, I rise up and wrap my hand around his throat, holding just tight enough for him to know I'm there. He doesn't flinch. Of course he doesn't.

"You're *mine*," I snarl. "I own you. I can do whatever I want to you."

"Yes, Daddy," he rasps, his gaze unblinking. I feel the words vibrating against my palm. My cock is throbbing harder in my pants.

If I stop to think about it, there would probably be a world of possibilities at my fingertips. So many wild things I could do with him. But I feel ravenous. I want him, *now*.

Honestly, when I'm with a pretty girl, I usually just stick to the front door because it's easiest and quickest. However, I can't deny there's a different kind of pleasure that comes from behind. It takes more patience and dedication, but when I've got a lifeless doll in my hands, I already know he's not going to get bored or impatient.

He's mine to do with as I please.

I fold him down right there on the carpet. From what I can tell out of the corner of my eye, the threesome seems to have reached its natural conclusion. I have a feeling the attention of the room might have shifted my way. I don't care. I'm safe here. It's been a very long time since I did anything so public. For some reason, it feels right to try something new out in the open.

After all, I wanted this night to be authentic. Right now, there's nowhere to hide. I've opened myself up to this new experience, and all these strangers are going to bear witness.

Considering how hard I am, it's not going to take long.

My doll is on all fours, his head slightly raised so I can see his face as he waits for my next move. I grab a throw pillow from my vacated armchair. I have no shame in my age, but I respect myself enough to know that my knees aren't what they used to be, and a little forethought will go a long way.

Positioning myself behind him, I kneel up and flick his robe and dress up over his hips. As I suspected, his under-wear is a jockstrap, so his hole is already gloriously exposed for me. I waste no time in ripping the lube packet open with my teeth and drizzling some over my fingers. I push my middle one against his fluttering ring, loving how he flexes and relaxes, letting me in relatively quickly.

I lean forward and wrap my free hand around his neck again, pulling up a little as I press my chest against his back. "I could fuck you all night," I growl, a rush of adrenaline coming purely from my words as they caress against the shell of his ear. "I can do anything. My pretty doll. I'm going to fuck you. I don't care if you come or not. You're here for my pleasure."

His lack of reaction fuels me, emboldens me. I've already got two fingers inside him, fucking his hole and stroking his prostate. It's strangely exhilarating that he's not reacting at all. *I'm* in control. *I* have all the power.

Unable to wait any longer, I withdraw, fumbling with my zipper to free myself. I have no idea how many people are watching us. It doesn't matter. All I care about is playing with my new toy. He chose me to give himself over to. Somehow, I earned this.

I promised myself I wouldn't waste this night, and I intend to honor that promise.

He swallows my cock, and the tight heat is heavenly, even with the condom on. It's been so long since I took this particular kind of pleasure from anyone. I can't help but drop my head back and moan, pushing deeper inside him, taking what's been given freely to me.

"Do you like that, doll?" I ask as I slowly start to rock back and forth, getting us both used to the sensation.

"I love it, Daddy," he says in that same calm tone of voice. I'd think he wasn't affected at all by my cock filling him up, but I can see the perspiration gathering on the small of his back. I massage my fingers against his neck, feeling him swallow and the dampness of his skin. I lean down and nuzzle my cheek against his again.

"Do you want more?" I snarl.

"Please, Daddy," he repeats.

It's strange how his stillness gives me confidence. This is what he asked for—what he wants. He's perfectly capable of stopping me with a single word or a tap of his hand, but he's just taking everything I give him.

I trust that he's enjoying it. I trust that we're on the same page. It makes it easy in the end to just let go and fuck him senseless.

My pants are pooled around my knees, my belt buckle jingling as I pound into my beautiful doll. I knew I wouldn't last long once I got to it, and I was right. My climax roars through me, shattering my world in an instant as I'm consumed by ecstasy.

As I gasp for breath, a part of me acknowledges that this is all I wanted. To come with no expectation of doing anything for my partner. I wanted to be a selfish, lazy bastard tonight, and I still say there's nothing wrong with that.

Expect it's not what I want anymore.

This is my doll, and he said I could play with him however I liked.

My cock softening inside him, I press my chest to his back again and hastily thrust my hand down his underwear, freeing his leaking, juicy cock, my fingers slick with the last of the lube. "Come for me, doll," I growl into his ear. "You're mine. Do as I say. Come for me now."

I detect just the faintest whimper and shiver down his spine as he explodes all over the floor. Jason and Markus will have a cleaning crew in as soon as everyone has left, so I don't feel too bad about the mess.

Instead, I hum and suck his neck as he spurts over and over. I forgot how satisfying it is to really *see* your partner orgasm. Don't get me wrong, I love making women come undone in rapid succession, something men can't do in the same way. But there's a different pleasure in feeling my victory in such a visceral manner.

I stroke him in a slightly gentler manner as he winds down, making sure to milk every last drop from him. On a whim, I lift my hand and press my fingers against his lips. "Be a good doll and suck me clean," I rasp, feeling dizzy on the high of my orgasm, not to mention the rush of power.

I watch in fascination as he does exactly that, licking and sucking each finger as well as my palm. But he keeps his gaze forward, focusing on nothing in particular and therefore still maintaining that air of an inanimate object. Even after coming my brains out, I find him intoxicating.

For the first time in a long time, I curse my age.

I want him again, now. Can I keep him here long enough to do that?

I guess there's only one way to find out.

CHAPTER 5

Kadence

A storm is raging inside me. A hurricane, even. But on the surface, my waters are smooth. Calm. Perfect.

I almost feel like I'm on the outside looking over myself as McKenna drapes his larger body over mine, panting, both our clothes damp, lubricant and semen dripping and drying all over the place.

When I'd come slinking up to him, fluttering my eyelashes, I was half convinced he was going to shoo me away. If not, I thought maybe he might take me to a private corner and fondle me up a little. Perhaps ask for a blow job.

Never in a million years did I truly believe he'd bend me over and fuck me in front of a room full of people like a rabid beast.

It was absolutely delicious.

God, it was almost *too* good. I forgot who I am, what I'm trying to achieve.

If only I'd had someone taking pictures. I doubt there would be an easy way to deny what just happened to the press. As it was…that was only between us. And a room full of kinksters, yes. But I'm not sure how I feel. I enjoyed it. I can't deny that. But…

But nothing. This is a long game. I've had plenty of good sex devoid of feelings. This man's son being a case in point. That trouble started *outside* the bedroom. Just because the chemistry between Daddy McKenna and me was immediately off the charts doesn't change my goal. In fact, I should view this as a delightful bonus on my quest for justice. Like dental care as part of your health insurance.

Lucky me.

"Are you still a doll?" McKenna murmurs against my ear. He's still inside me, his hand still cupping my spent cock. He caresses the backs of his clean fingers against my cheek.

"I'm always a doll, Daddy," I say cheekily. "But I was done being in doll mode unless you want to keep playing."

His breath is warm on my neck as he nuzzles his nose against my damp hair. He inhales deeply and hums. "I think I want you to be a boy again. If that's how this works."

"It can be whatever you want," I assure him.

"I like you talking," he says. I feel his words reverberating from his chest against my back. "But stay still for me, Kiki. Don't move until I say."

I hum in response, indicating that I'll do as he's asked.

There's movement all around the room. Quiet music is playing, and people are talking and making sensual noises. We're no longer the center of attention. I still can't believe that Daddy McKenna willingly did that. Perhaps my honey trap isn't going to be so difficult to set, after all.

Gently he eases out of me. I don't look around, staying still like he asked. I'm not quite in doll mode anymore. The head space has shifted, and I've lost that dreamy, floaty feeling. I'm surprised how well he was able to take me there for his first time. But it's easy for me to lock my muscles and play the part. Sometimes it's actually a struggle to become inanimate. That can either be frustrating or part of the fun depending on who I'm with. But right now, I just lock my limbs and let my gaze settle in the middle distance.

I'm not sure what I'm expecting. I think I feel him rearranging himself behind me, and most likely hear the chink of his metal belt buckle. It's a bit difficult to be sure with all the other movements and noises around me. Someone I don't know strokes my hair as they walk past me. I like that.

What I thought he'd do was maybe give me a rimming. Some guys like admiring their handiwork up close and personal afterward. And I know he's approaching fifty, so therefore unlikely to get it up again anytime soon. But the other thing I thought he might do while my body was still his to control was perhaps settle back in his armchair and get me to warm his cock until he was ready to fuck my face.

When the slightly cold baby wipe slides along my crack, it takes everything I've got to not jump a foot in the air.

"Good doll," he says warmly as he cleans me up. He mops up around my cock and slips me back into my underwear. Then he gently pulls my dress and robe back down before running his hand lightly along my back, over my ass, and down the back of my thigh.

My chest tightens. What's he doing? He's a bastard with a bastard son. He's not supposed to be tender.

I'm so shocked that I'm not aware as he moves around me until he wraps his hand around my elbow and helps me stand. I'm ashamed to say that I wobble a little on my three-inch heels, but he's right there, still gripping my arm to make sure I don't fall.

This is the first time we've stood next to each other. I'm slightly taller thanks to my shoes, but he doesn't seem bothered. In fact, he's still radiating that Daddy Dom confidence that I was drawn to in the first place.

"Come sit with me some more," he says, stepping back

toward the armchair that respectfully no one took while he was otherwise occupied. His fingers are still strong against my elbow, so I naturally follow his lead.

But my heart is beating faster, and a feeling like panic is prickling over my skin. My instinct is screaming at me that this is enough, even though I'm not sure why. My plan is working even better than I'd hoped. Yet something in me is saying I need to quit while I'm ahead.

"Sorry, Daddy," I say, resisting his pull just a fraction. It's remarkable how he stops tugging me right away. I bat my eyelashes and go for my signature cute-but-bratty attitude. "Kiki-rella has to leave before midnight, I'm afraid."

He raises his eyebrows. "I don't want you to leave."

It's interesting that he doesn't say it in a threatening way. Actually, his disappointment is flattering. Or it would be if I was genuinely interested in him. All it really means is that I've done a good job seducing him, and I feel a savage rush of satisfaction.

I pout and tap his nose. "Sorry, Daddy," I say again. "I had fun, though."

Now, this is where I need to gamble. I *have* to make him think this is his idea. Time to see if I've done enough to have him craving another round. For whatever reason, I know I need to leave. It's probably because I know if I give him too much now, that'll be it forever. No chance to take photos and enact my revenge. So I slip out of his grasp, pick my purse up off the floor where I left it, and begin to walk away, swishing my robe, knowing his eyes will be on my bare ass which is concealing my throbbing, well-fucked hole.

Three…two…

"Wait!"

I take a breath and school my features before peeking back over my shoulder. He's got his hands in his pockets and his eyes are narrowed at me. There are a few feet between us, but the other patrons seem to sense not to walk between us as we stare at one another.

"Do you really have to go?" he asks eventually.

"Yes," I say simply.

It's a good thing that I don't owe him an explanation, because I can't really give him one. I'm not entirely sure myself. I'd planned on staying at the party for several hours. I could go and make him jealous with some other guy or guys. But honestly, all I want right now is to get in my car and head home.

I respect the fact that he doesn't ask me why. He just tilts his head and licks his lips, his gaze boring into me. Needless to say, his pants are back on and he's looking dignified again in his fancy suit. I love that he fucked me in that. He didn't even take his jacket off. The man radiates power, and I've got him looking at me with confusion and uncertainty.

It's intoxicating.

He seems to be wrestling with himself, but finally, he speaks. "Can I see you again?"

My heart leaps. *Yes!* My plan is working! I'm far too much of a pro to show anything on my face that I don't want to, but I do grace him with just a twitch of a smile.

"Maybe," I say. "Are you local?"

"Yes," he says.

Smart. I might have got him punch drunk on me, but he's not so stupid as to blurt out his address in the open. The thing is, I know he's based in Albertson, which is the next big town over from Paddle Creek. But *he* doesn't know that I know that.

"Are you going to spoil me?" I ask, fluttering my eyelashes and taking a step closer to him. I clutch my fluffy purse in both hands over my belly button, using it as a minimalist shield. He's got to work to entice me, and he knows it.

"Yes," he replies simply to my question. "I'll send a car for you, and we can play again. If that's something you're interested in."

I tap my chin and pretend to think about it. "Will you buy me a present?"

It's him who takes a step closer this time. He doesn't hesitate as he lifts his arm and slips his hand around my throat. The move is both somehow gentle but firm. I gasp, just a little.

"I take *very* good care of all my toys, Kiki," he says, his voice rich and smooth like expensive coffee. He rubs his thumb against my pulse point. "Let Daddy play with you again, and I'll shower you with presents."

I take a couple of shaky breaths. This close, I can see that his eyes are a dark forest green with crinkles around them, showing his maturity. Fucking hell, he's not so much hot as so classically handsome it makes me want to worship at his feet.

It's a good thing that's exactly what he wants as well.

"I'll give you my number, Daddy," I purr. "You just tell me where and when, and Kiki will be the prettiest, most perfect doll for you."

He licks his lips and looks down at mine. For a heart-stopping moment I worry he's going to try and kiss me. That's definitely off the cards. I never actually kissed his good-for-nothing son, after all. But instead, he nods.

I take it as my cue to step back, and he releases his hold on me right away. Glancing around, I spy a pile of napkins. Perfect. Reaching down, I pluck one up, making sure to stick my ass out as I do. Then I pop open my purse, extract my lipstick, and press the napkin to McKenna's chest.

"Stay still," I rasp.

I feel him watching me as I write my digits on the tissue paper in bright red. Then I fold it over and tuck it into his breast pocket before tapping his chest.

"Bye, Daddy," I say with a wink, clicking the lipstick lid back on, dropping it back in my purse, and sauntering away.

I just know he hates to say good-bye but loves to watch me leave.

Hopefully that means it won't take him long to call me. The clock is ticking, and this doll is ready for revenge *now*.

CHAPTER 6

Rafferty

Jason and Markus's party was days ago. I really shouldn't be giving it much of a second thought beyond the invigoration it gave me.

But I can't get a certain pretty doll out of my head.

A *boy,* no less. A young man. The ass-fucking wasn't all that unusual, but the fact that I eagerly jerked him off is a brand-new one on me.

I guess that's why my mind keeps drifting back to the short but gripping encounter. It's forcing me to ask a couple of pretty fundamental questions about myself. All I can say is that in almost fifty years, I've never once been swept away by another man. Those couple of guys in college pursued me, and I figured life's too short not to try most things once. But…well, they were both effeminate. Very. In fact, one of them was such a beautiful drag queen he could have almost passed as a woman.

So…it's not like I'm suddenly gay, that's for sure. But perhaps I am the slightest bit bisexual? Or maybe there's an even better word. It seems like there's a label for everything these days. I'm still definitely attracted to beauty. But it turns out that maybe I don't care so much what's between the other person's legs.

I realize someone else around the boardroom table has begun to speak, and I give myself a mental slap. In all honestly, I don't especially need to pay attention to what's being discussed. It's just a lot of my department heads patting themselves on the back for another successful quarter. But this is my company, and I need to at least feign I give a shit what these people are saying.

Christ, it's like being back at that fundraiser. I'm sure everyone here is genuinely happy that they're just that bit richer than they were yesterday. But it all feels painfully false. I'm sure no one here actually *likes* each other. I can hardly remember all their names, for crying out loud.

I know Kiki's name.

No, I don't. I can't help but snort, earning a raised eyebrow from my executive assistant, Audrey, who's meant to be taking notes, even though there isn't much really going on. I ignore her, pretending it never happened. She's far too savvy to let me gaslight her into anything, so I don't feel too bad. However, she's also known me long enough to know that I'll never explain anything that I don't want to.

Like how I'm fantasizing over a pretty doll whose last name I don't know. I'm sure he just uses Kiki for playtime. So I have no actual name I could search for to get any further information. Nothing I could run a background check on.

I have hook-ups with strangers all the time. Like Charleen so coldly pointed out, I never lead them on or think there could be a relationship. That's not what I'm looking for, so I rarely give the encounters a second thought other than to replay the delicious memories for my own pleasure.

I don't wonder what they're doing now. I don't wonder what their job is or who the important people are in their lives. And I certainly don't wonder if I should call them for a repeat performance.

Never have I ever slept with the same person twice except Charleen, nor have I even wanted to. But it's as if Kiki's number is burning a hole in my pocket. Somewhat literally, as I've kept the napkin he gave me on my person ever since. It's currently on the inside of my jacket, and I rub the spot absently, like I'm soothing a wounded heart.

Now that is ridiculous. It's not like I'm pining after such a brief encounter. I'm just…lusting after something gorgeous. I didn't get to be this insanely wealthy without being just a little greedy, obviously. I'm not satisfied. I want Kiki again, that's all. I experienced something entirely new and exciting with him, not like the usual young women I bed. It's going to be a lot harder to chase what we shared with someone else.

Besides, I don't want to. I don't have to.

Perhaps it's time to admit to myself that it's not a matter of 'if' I contact him, but 'when.' I'm just trying to play it cool with how quickly I make the call. I don't want to give my power away by seeming desperate. Again, a tactic I'm well aware of after so many years in business.

But also the thought of anyone else touching Kiki in the time it takes me to reach out makes me want to throw something.

He's *mine.* The control he gave me was intoxicating. In some ways, I've never felt that close to anyone in my life, and yet I know we barely scratched the surface of what we could have done. I want to play with him a lot more, and until I get him out of my system, I don't want anybody else putting their hands on what's mine.

Just in time, I realize that my CFO has glanced my way and said my name, no doubt handing the meeting back to me so I can close it. Without missing a beat, I rattle off the few statements I prepared in advance about our recent achievements but with confident assurances that in the following months we can do even better. There's a round of applause that I do my best to only cringe internally at, then I'm finally free.

"Good weekend, sir?" Audrey murmurs at me as she closes her laptop. We're the last to leave the room, and I know she's taking the chance to be cheeky and push our boundaries.

I simply give her a cool look before standing and buttoning my suit jacket. "I expect those meeting minutes typed up and emailed to all parties within the hour," I tell her.

My assistant scoffs and stands herself. "Who do you think I am? They'll be out in twenty minutes." She picks up her computer and winks at me.

I merely hum in response. But just before she reaches the door, I change my mind and find something I want to ask, after all. "Is there another meeting booked in here for now?"

She pauses at the threshold. "There is now, Mr. McKenna," she says with a grin, then closes the door behind her.

Warring with myself for a second, I unbutton my jacket once more and sit back down. The internal glass is frosted, so people might see a dark blur in here if they look closely, but otherwise, I actually have more privacy now than I would in my office. At least for a few minutes.

I pull out my phone, my only plan being to finally input Kiki's number into it. I'd been holding off, like that might somehow take some of the magic away from our encounter. But suddenly, I quite urgently feel the need to make it real. However, I'm made to stop before I can retrieve the napkin by a message I've received from my wife.

CHARLEEN: Moved my LA trip up, leaving today. Not due back until mid-August. Call if you need anything. And behave.

I scoff again, far louder this time. The audacity of that woman. She's off to fuck her bit on the side, and she expects me to behave?

I was intending on doing the opposite but now I'm going to misbehave even harder out of spite.

It takes no time at all to punch in Kiki's number and fire off a message.

RAFFERTY: Hello, Kiki. It's Daddy. Is now a good time to talk?

I'm prepared to have to wait a considerable time for a response. I have no idea what his job is or if he's allowed to keep his phone on his person. He could be in a meeting. He could still be a student and be sitting in a lecture. I feel a little uneasy at the idea of him being that young. My own son has only just graduated from college, after all.

Oh, for heaven's sake. It's not like me to doubt myself like this. We're two consenting adults, that's all that matters. He might not even have been sincere about wanting to play again. What is it the kids say these days? He could 'leave me on read,' and I'll never get the chance to find out what job he does or even what his real name is.

Before I can tie myself up in knots, the seen icon appears, and three little dots bounce, indicating he's typing. Thank goodness. I was on the verge of becoming unhinged over a young man I met for all of thirty minutes.

KIKI: Give me a second, Daddy.

He adds a kissing face emoji. It's crazy how fast my heart is beating. I try and wait patiently, but I find myself nibbling on my thumbnail, something I haven't done in years.

The ringtone makes me jump, despite hoping that's exactly what he was doing. I take a breath and force myself to hold off answering for a couple of seconds, not wanting to appear too needy.

I genuinely don't recognize who I am right now.

"Hello," I say smoothly.

He makes a noise that's like a cross between a groan and a purr. The sound is kind of echoey, and I wonder if he's slipped into the bathroom so we can talk.

I like that. I want him all to myself.

"Hi, Daddy," he says playfully. "I've been waiting for you to call me. Did you miss me?"

"Yes," I say simply, not bothering to lie.

He chuckles. "Me, too."

I believe him.

"What are you doing right now?" I ask. I'm fully aware that the appeal of parties like the other night is to have anonymous fun. But I don't care. I want to know about his life.

He groans, and not the sexy kind. "I'm at my boring new job. It's only been a couple of weeks, and I'm already tearing my hair out. But I just graduated, and I need to pay the bills, so I took the first thing that came my way."

I chuckle at his whining. I enjoy a petulant brat. They all secretly want a firm hand to keep them in line, and I'm more than happy to oblige them.

"What do you do?" I ask, indulging him in a little chit-chat.

"My official title is office bitch," he says completely deadpan.

"Of course it is," I tease him back. I can tell how much I'm smiling, and it would be unsettling if I didn't feel the most relaxed and playful I have in a very long time.

"It is!" he squeaks indignantly. "It says so on my business cards. Or it would if I was important enough to have any."

So I've got some answers. He's graduated and is working an entry-level position that he doesn't give a shit about. I want to ask him what he *really* wants to do, but not over the phone. What I really want to do is give us the opportunity to have that kind of conversation later.

"What are you doing this weekend, Kiki?" I ask bluntly. I don't know how long he'll be able to hide in the men's room, and I don't want to miss the opportunity of setting something up with him.

There's a slight pause before he lets out a very enticing breath. "You, hopefully, Daddy," he rasps.

Well, I walked right into that one, didn't I? I smirk, not regretting it one bit as I rearrange myself so my thickening cock doesn't become uncomfortable.

"Correct answer, baby doll," I say, my voice low and full of promise.

Over the past few days, whenever I'd imagined seeing Kiki again, I'd planned on taking him to a hotel. But now that the perfect scenario has fallen into my lap, I fully intend on making the most of it.

There is a small voice in the back of my mind, though, that gives me pause. How much of my life do I want to share with this kinky little minx? If this goes sour, I have about a thousand percent more to lose than he does.

In that moment, however, I remember that what brought me here was an overpowering desire for authenticity. If I'm going to do this, I don't see any point in holding back. It's not like I intend on giving the boy my bank details, but I also don't particularly feel like sneaking around at hotels, either. Besides, not only would that increase our potential of being seen by someone who might question the nature of our relationship, it would also limit our time together.

I don't want another brief fling.

I want to indulge.

"What naughty things did you have in mind, Daddy?" he prompts me.

"Give me an address you'd like to be picked up from," I

tell him. "I'll send a driver to collect you on Friday evening. If all goes well, I want you to be mine until Sunday night."

There's a *whoosh* down the line as he exhales. For a second, I worry that I might have pushed him too far and asked too much. Then I chide myself for this irritating insecurity I keep displaying. I've told him what I want. If that's not in line with his desires, he's free to let me know. This is all completely consensual, after all.

"Oh, *Daddy*," he whispers. "We're going to have so much fun. I hope you're going to buy me some nice things, too, like you promised. I'll be your perfect doll. You can play with me however you want. I'm yours."

Christ, I'm not going to be able to leave this meeting room anytime soon, am I? I press the heel of my palm against my throbbing cock. But it doesn't do much good. My imagination is already running away thinking about all the delicious things I want to do to that boy's beautiful body.

"Are you going to be pretty for Daddy?" I murmur.

"So pretty," he hisses like a snake. It makes me think of an anaconda. He's wrapping himself around me, and I'm just letting him squeeze me for all I've got with absolutely no regrets.

I'll spoil him. I'll pamper him. I don't care if he's using me, because we're being honest and I'm using him right back. There's no way an arrangement like this can last very long, so I intend to play the game every second I can.

Down the line, I hear voices and the banging of a door. "I've got to go, Daddy," he whispers so quietly I barely hear him. God, that turns me on. He's my beautiful dirty secret, and only mine.

"Good boy," I tell him softly. "Text me the address you want to be picked up from, and Daddy will take care of everything."

He giggles before ending the call. The sudden silence in

the room envelops me, but I quite like being alone with just my thoughts for a moment. This gorgeous creature is giving himself over to me for two days and nights. I will own him as my toy to pleasure myself with. The rush of power and dominance does nothing to help with my raging erection.

Without overthinking it, I grab my folio that will serve as enough of a protective shield to get me back to my office so hopefully no one will notice my predicament. Then I'm locking myself in my private bathroom, where my right hand and I are going to have a one-to-one so I can start planning just exactly how I'm going to enjoy my beautiful doll this weekend.

CHAPTER 7

Kadence

I can't believe this is actually working. I'm giddy with excitement. This is exactly the kind of opportunity I was looking for. McKenna is bringing me to his goddamned *house.* I thought he might want a quickie at a hotel at most. But this is next level. I'm going to be able to get so much dirt on him.

Plus, you know, he's hot. He's clearly not new to being dominant, and I don't think I'm the first person to call him 'Daddy.' But for someone who says he didn't know what it meant to have a doll to play with, he certainly took to it fast. Oh, yeah. This bastard likes to control things. Let's see how out of control he feels when I splash all his dirty laundry all over the internet.

"If you don't text me regularly," Jessie threatens beside me, "I'm calling Sheriff Chancey. No, I'll get Nim to rally the Cardinals, and we'll just storm the building and drag you out, understood?"

I chuckle and wrap my arm around my friend. We're standing outside Toe Beans, the cat café his Daddy, Nim, owns. The Cardinals are his biker family, and it wouldn't be the first time they'd joined forces to rescue a boy, from what I've heard. So I don't doubt Jessie's sincerity.

"I'll be fine," I assure him yet again. "But yes, I promise I'll keep in touch so you know I haven't been murdered by the scary stranger."

I haven't told my friends everything. They certainly don't know that my new sugar Daddy is Logan's father or that I'm planning on ruining the entire family's reputation just to get back at my ex-fuck buddy. But Jessie does know that I'm being whisked away for a weekend of sin by my new amour that I met at the party I went to.

I secretly love that he's worried about me, but it's not something I'm used to. My parents haven't reached out once to check that I'm still alive since I left home, simply relying on hearing occasionally from my sister that we're both okay. Jessie's concern makes me feel awkward and itchy.

Instead of trying to articulate how I'm feeling, I simply hug him tighter and kiss his cheek. A shiny black car is approaching, and I glance at the number plate to confirm it's the one McKenna sent for me.

I'm fully aware that my intentions with this man are nefarious. But it is pretty awesome that he insisted on having me picked up from a public place to respect the privacy of my home. Jessie agreed that was a bit assuring, along with the fact that we met at a very public party. But he's still fretting that it might have all been a ploy and that my date could still be a serial killer. McKenna might be a bastard, but I think I'm going to be safe enough at his house.

"I'll give you all the juicy details when I get home, okay?" I promise my friend.

He grins at me. "I wouldn't expect anything less."

The car pulls up to the curb, and a suited driver gets out to open the back door for me. A flash of nerves surges through me, but I'm not sure why. I've got this. I give Jessie a goofy thumbs-up, then get inside the vehicle. Operation Fuck Over Logan McKenna has officially entered phase two.

It's only about a twenty-minute drive to Albertson, but we don't go into the town center. I tried to find any information about McKenna's home online, but he's got good privacy set up—for now, at least. I'm not surprised, however, that he's gotten a mansion in the middle of nowhere. It's a pretty standard looking house, except that it's three stories high and twice the width of a regular home.

It doesn't stir much within me, but I can't help but admire the sweeping gravel driveway and the white ornamental fountain in front of the building. Half a dozen perfectly manicured shrubs sit in pristine white pots between the columns that stand at the house's entrance. They're not holding up anything other than the extended roof. Mostly, they're just decorative.

It's a preposterous waste of wealth. A pure display of power. I wouldn't expect anything else, but it is a little disappointing that this man is as clichéd as I assumed he was. After all, this is the kind of world I come from. Money doesn't impress me.

Kindness does.

I need to remember that he might be a smoking silver fox and the one time we've fucked so far was incredible. But when everything's said and done, he's still a soulless millionaire. He's leaving Paddle Creek to slowly decay while he lives up life here.

Shaking myself, I push those thoughts aside. They're not going to be helpful in my quest for justice. I need to keep my eye on the prize and not let my heart get invested. It shouldn't be too difficult. After the way I allowed his son to get to me, I've sworn off feelings even harder than before.

And it's not because I think I'm unlovable.

Probably.

The driver gets my case out of the trunk. I packed a *lot*. I might only be here for a couple of days, but McKenna specifically wanted me to be pretty for him, so I needed to make sure I had plenty of options available to me.

The more I think about it, the more I feel like McKenna leans toward the straight end of the Kinsey scale. I couldn't care less what anyone's sexual preferences are so long as they're not hurting anyone, and I won't stand for any kind of bisexual shaming or the like. But if he needs me to give him more of a feminine illusion for my plan to keep working, I'm happy to indulge him.

It's not like it's a bad thing for me, anyway. I love an excuse to get glammed up. And I hate guys who fem-shame. So I might not be in doll mode as I approach the front door, but I've got on a cute shift dress, cinched in with a chunky belt, and a pair of ankle boots. I'm wearing day make-up, so it still took a lot of effort on my part, but your average guy would probably only notice the glossy lips and eyeliner.

I'm here to be this man's doll for the weekend. His fantasy. He doesn't need to know how much work went into looking perfect for him.

McKenna instructed me to go ahead and ring the doorbell when I arrived. By the time I get to the top of the stone steps, the car is already pulling away, the gravel crunching under the tires until it disappears out of sight. Exhaling, I turn back and steel myself before pressing the bell.

"You've got this," I murmur. If I just switch off the reasons why I'm here in the first place, there's a strong chance I'm going to have a lot of fun.

I don't have to wait long before the door opens inward, and there he is. Fuck, he is handsome. Chiseled jawline, tanned skin, salt-and-pepper hair, and big strong hands. He's not wearing a jacket today, but he's still dressed in a light blue shirt with the top couple of buttons undone, navy slacks, and gentlemanly house slippers.

"Hello, *Daddy*," I say appreciatively.

He smirks at me and licks his lips. "Hello, beautiful," he greets me back. "Thank you for coming. Let me get that for you."

I don't try and stop him as he slides his fingers around my suitcase handle. It's not exactly empty, so I like it that he picks it up easily. Just as I thought, he's still in good shape. And he might be an arrogant, rich asshole, but a little chivalry goes a long way in my book.

"Thank you," I simper, fluttering my eyelashes at him.

His gaze lingers on my mouth for just a second too long for it to go unnoticed. Then he clears his throat and indicates with his free hand for me to head inside. I step over the threshold, and he closes the door. As soon as it clicks shut, he wraps his hand around my stomach, pressing his chest to my back as he nuzzles his nose against my neck and inhales deeply. I'm really glad I used my special occasion expensive perfume and moisturizer so that I smell extra yummy for him.

"We're alone," he murmurs against my skin. "I dismissed the weekend staff."

"Your family?" I ask. I want him to know I am not some naïve little thing.

He grunts and presses a kiss to my neck. "Also not here and not coming back for a long time."

I already know where Logan lives as that's where he used to fuck me. Morbid curiosity wants me to push to ask about McKenna's wife. He's still wearing a wedding ring, after all. But she's not my problem. Anyway, she married this man, and Logan is her son as well. I don't feel any particular sympathy for her or the fact that I'm planning on humiliating her as much as Logan and his father. They're all as bad as each other, as far as I'm concerned.

McKenna's hand travels farther down, slipping under the bottom of my dress and fondling the globes of my ass. Normally, I'd have worn a jock-strap for him so he could have easy access, but I didn't want to flash anyone in town without their consent. Still, I picked out some of my fanciest underwear for him to discover as a treat. I moan and lean more against him, my eyes fluttering closed as he continues around my hips and presses his palm over my hardening length.

"Love that you're wearing lace," he says, nipping at my earlobe.

"Of course, Daddy," I say. "I told you I'd be pretty for you. What are you going to do to your new toy?"

He growls, biting down on my lobe before releasing me. "Everything. Come this way."

He places his hand on the small of my back and takes my suitcase handle once again. Then he ushers me up a staircase made of dark, shiny wood that curves along the wall and around to the second floor. There are gray rugs on the wooden floors and the walls are painted a tasteful sage green.

We soon enter a bedroom decorated mostly in peach tones with an honest-to-god chandelier hanging from the ceiling. I spy an enormous built-in closet with white wooden doors and a large white dressing table with lightbulbs around the mirror like a starlet's dressing room might have. A balcony opens up to look over the grounds, and there's a door to an en suite. From this angle, the bathroom looks bigger than my whole room back at the apartment, but I'll have to investigate that later when McKenna leaves me alone. This space has a beautiful feminine energy to it that I appreciate. I can see myself lounging around here draped in silks and ostrich feathers.

"This will be your room, Kiki," McKenna informs me as he places my bag at the foot of the bed. "You will not venture any farther down the corridor or go upstairs. You will stick to here and downstairs."

"Yes, Daddy," I assure him. Yeah, I know it doesn't make any sense if I'm here to ruin his family name, but until then, I can respect his privacy.

"I will come in here and fuck you whenever I please," he continues, grinding all my other thoughts to a halt. "You will be my doll for the entirety of your stay. Unless you use your safewords, I will play with you however I like. Your orgasms belong to me. You are not allowed to come until I tell you to. You are absolutely not allowed to touch yourself unless it's for my viewing pleasure and I instruct you to. You are to be beautiful for me at all times. You will call me Daddy, and for as long as you are here, you will love your Daddy with all your porcelain heart. I will feed you and take care of you. The closet is filled with new clothes that you are to wear for your Daddy. If I don't tell you what I want you to be in, you have my permission to decide what I think I will like the most. You will exist for my pleasure until I release you on Sunday. Do you understand?"

My heart is racing in my chest and my half-hard cock has visibly thickened to full mast under my dress. I've already slipped into doll mode, allowing my gaze to un-focus, and my arms are hanging in neutral by my sides.

"Yes, Daddy," I say in my doll voice.

He steps back over to me, running his hands over my skin and kissing my neck again. "Good doll," he says quietly. I'm already drifting away, letting everything go. What happens next isn't up to me. I give myself freely to this man.

His hands are back under my dress, skimming over my panties. But this time he wastes no time in peeling them off, pushing them down until they fall around my ankles.

"You are to be ready for your Daddy at all times," he says, licking the shell of my ear. "I will pleasure you, but only if you pleasure Daddy first. I won't fuck around with too many layers of clothing when I want to play."

"Yes, Daddy," I reply automatically.

He's stroking my dick, rubbing his thumb over the head, and it's taking more effort than usual not to tremble. I feel like melting into a puddle, but I have to stay strong for him. Usually, it's easy for me to disassociate. In fact, that's the whole appeal of doll play. But this man makes me want to scream and beg.

I'm not supposed to be feeling anything at all, though, so I fall back on my doll phrases to try and hurry this first session along. I'm overwhelmed with his intoxicating dominance, and I'm going to need some time alone to get my shit together if I'm going to survive this intense weekend. If I satisfy him, hopefully, he'll leave me alone to shower and settle in. I can use that time to collect myself.

This is a job, after all. Not a date.

"I love you, Daddy," I say. Sure enough, that elicits a filthy moan from him.

"Get on your knees, doll," he rasps.

There's another rug in here, but I would have bruised my knees for him, anyway. He needs to know he has complete control over me so he trusts me. I kick away my panties before I sink down, using my core to keep my movements as mechanical as possible. As he's still behind me, I blink a few times. When he can see me, I'll do my best not to move at all to further the illusion.

I remain motionless as he comes and stands in front of me, already unzipping his pants. Part of our deal is no condoms. I'm on PrEP in any case, but he also showed me his latest medical records and insisted I do the same. He's probably just covering his own ass so he doesn't give his wife something nasty, but I have to say it'll be a thrill to fuck bareback as it's something I never do.

He's been inside me before, but this is the first time I've seen his cock up close and personal. It's red and straining, precum already smeared over the bulbous head, the dark vein pronounced, balls large and heavy. I love that his length is nestled in graying dark curls and protruding through his pants and the bottom of his shirt. He's asserting his dominance by keeping his clothes on.

Gripping the back of my head with one hand, he holds his member with the other and rubs the tip against my lips. "You're so pretty," he mumbles as he begins pushing inside my mouth. Obediently, I wrap my lips around him, licking with my tongue and sucking him deeper. The rest of my body is motionless, though. Lifeless for him to do with as he pleases. He drops his head back as he starts to thrust deeper. "Good doll," he mutters. "Like that. Suck on Daddy's big cock. Such a pretty doll. All mine. Mine to fuck whenever I fucking want."

Spit is dripping down my chin. I take long, slow breaths through my nose as I suck and swallow and worship his dick. His fingers tighten in my hair, the pain sending a sharp jolt of pleasure through my body and making my balls throb.

He gnashes his teeth, and I prepare myself to take his load, but he suddenly withdraws and starts jerking off frantically in front of my face. Within seconds, he's coming with a roar, his cum splattering my face, my hair, and my clothes. I'm impressed at how much he paints me with, his hand flying over his length as he spits more and more cream all over me, claiming me, marking me as his own.

I absolutely love it when men get feral. I've turned this slick gentleman into a goddamned caveman.

Eventually, he slows down, milking the last few drips that

leak onto his fingers. Like last time, he holds his hand out to me, watching as I suck them clean.

Breathing heavily, he tucks himself back into his pants and zips himself up again, all the while never taking his eyes off me. I'm still looking into the middle distance, so I sense most of his movements from the corner of my eye rather than actually seeing them. But I know that I've got him enraptured.

He cups my face and rubs his thumb over my cheek, smearing his cum over my skin. "Beautiful," he murmurs.

Without saying anything else, he takes a firm hold of my shoulders and pulls me until I rise to my feet again. I'm still fully dressed apart from my underwear. He kneels down and undoes my boots, slipping my bare feet out. Then he places his hand on the small of my back again, guiding me toward the bed.

First, he kicks off his slippers and settles himself down, spreading his legs out in a V shape. Then he encircles my wrist with his fingers and tugs me, settling me with my back pressed against his chest, tapping his hand in between my legs so I open them as well. Then he flips up my dress, exposing my cock in all its leaking, throbbing glory.

"So beautiful," he mumbles against my ear.

I feel him lean over and hear a drawer open. A clicking noise suggests some kind of lid opening, and the scent of peaches fills the air, matching the room's décor. The lube is cold as he glides his hand over my dick, but I don't react in any way, staring determinedly ahead.

"Daddy loves his new Kiki toy," he says as he begins working me, the squelching sounding debaucherous. "Does Kiki love his Daddy?"

"I love you, Daddy," I reply automatically.

He hums and kisses my neck as he plays more with my dick. "I like this part of my toy. I like that I can see how excited Daddy makes his Kiki doll. Does Kiki like Daddy playing with him like this?"

"I love it, Daddy," I tell him, and fuck it, I'm not lying. I lie still as he jerks me off, his other hand slipping under my dress, groping and squeezing my pec, rubbing his thumb over my budded nipple.

"Such pretty little titties, all for Daddy," he mumbles. "Daddy is going to play with every single inch of his Kiki doll's body. Kiki looks so pretty covered in cum. That's what you were made for, wasn't it, Kiki? For Daddy to fuck you over and over and over."

"Yes, Daddy," I utter.

He's teasing me, slowing down before speeding up again, bringing me to the edge, only to pull me back once more.

"Does Kiki want to come?" he asks.

"Yes, Daddy," I reply, only just stopping my voice from cracking.

"Beg for it, Kiki. Tell Daddy how much you want to come all over yourself. Tell Daddy how much you love it. Kiki isn't allowed to come until Daddy says so, remember?"

I'm trying not to breathe too hard, but it's becoming more difficult. "Yes, Daddy," I utter, clinging to my composure by my fingertips. "Please, Daddy. I love you, Daddy. Please, Daddy. Please, please, please."

He speeds up, taking his hand out of my dress and instead pressing it on my stomach, his fingers digging against my flesh through my clothes. "Come for Daddy, Kiki. Show Daddy how much you love him. Daddy's perfect, beautiful doll."

I have to grit my teeth to stop myself from screaming or flailing about as I let go, my orgasm crashing through me as I explode all over his hand. I shoot over the blanket that's on top of the duvet. I might be still, but my cock is jerking in his fist like a fish caught on a line. My cum hits his pants and my clothes as well, spurting like a geyser as my balls empty every last drop.

"Good doll." McKenna purrs into my ear as I flop against him. "So beautiful. You were perfect, Kiki. Daddy loved it. Good doll. Well done. Daddy's so proud of you. Stay here with Daddy for just a bit longer. Then Daddy can clean up his precious Kiki doll, okay?"

He kisses my neck tenderly and gently wraps his arms around me. It feels…real. Like he genuinely treasured what we just shared. My heart is still racing, but I blink as I come back to myself, chest heaving as I pant.

I'm completely washed out, my emotions raw and unruly. I'm not supposed to be feeling anything outside of physical sensations, but it's like he's stripped me naked, and now there's nowhere to hide. I know part of this is a chemical come down after the euphoric high he just gave me, but it's overwhelming, and I can't seem to get a grip on myself.

He's supposed to fuck me, then leave me the fuck alone. Why is he still here? Why is he holding me like we're lovers? Why does he want to clean me up again? I can't breathe. I can't see. I…I…

I burst into tears.

CHAPTER 8

Rafferty

One moment I'm blissed out and sleepy. The next I am wide awake, trying to work out what the fuck just happened.

"Kiki, what the—?"

"Let me go," he says, trying to fight his way out of my arms. His dress has fallen down, covering him once again. We're smeared with a mixture of both our cum. He's gasping for breath as he thrashes against me, and suddenly, I realize how serious this is.

"Kiki, *stop!*" I shout, locking my arms around his body and throwing one of my legs over his. "Calm down and listen to me." He tries in vain to struggle for a few more seconds, then he goes limp in my arms. "Good boy," I murmur against his ear.

I start breathing slowly and deeply, waiting for him to mimic me. Again, he resists to start with, but eventually, I've got him inhaling a decent amount of oxygen at the same time as I do.

"Right," I say when I think he's calmed down a reasonable amount. "Do you want to tell me what's wrong?"

He shakes his head vehemently. I don't like it, but I can tell bullying him probably isn't going to yield any answers. I chew my lip for a moment, thinking about the best tactic.

"Did *I* do something wrong?" My instinct doesn't feel like I did, but I am new to this particular kink, after all.

He takes too long a pause before shaking his head again, this time slower.

I grit my teeth. "Kiki, if I fucked up, you need to tell me."

This pause is even longer. Just when I'm starting to get mad, though, he finally speaks. "You didn't," he croaks.

I sigh, not believing him. "Okay, I think we need a new rule. And that's when Daddy asks you a question, you have to be honest with me. I know this is your kink, but I do understand that this is one hell of a power imbalance. We've got to be able to trust each other. So I'm going to ask you again. What's wrong? I assume it's not normal for you to become hysterical after a scene."

"Normally, I just leave," he spits out, trying halfheartedly to pull away from me once more.

I just hold him tighter, resting my temple against the top of his head while I think. *Ahhh.* Something clicks into place. He rushed off after our first encounter as well.

Until now, I might not have had a wealth of kinky encounters. But I know that after rough sex, it's important to me to tend to my partner, cleaning them and making them feel cherished. Otherwise, it can fuck with their heads. I think the official term for that is aftercare.

It seems perhaps my pretty doll isn't used to that.

"Are you upset because I said I was going to look after you?" I ask.

I feel him cringe against me. Bingo.

Well, my first instinct is rage. I know this young man isn't really mine, but right now, he belongs to me, and I don't like the idea of other people mistreating my property in the slightest. But whoever those assholes are who didn't see to him after they'd used him, they aren't here now. Kiki is, and that's all I really care about.

"Kiki," I say gently as I rub his arm and kiss his hair. "This is going to be another of our rules. You will let me take care of you after we have sex and, actually, whenever I damn well see fit. You asked to be spoiled, and that doesn't just mean pretty clothes. That means you will let me hold you and clean you and tell you that you did well. Do you think you can accept that?"

Another pause. This one doesn't last as long before he's turning his shimmering eyes on me. "Why?" he whispers.

I frown. "Why what?"

He licks his lips and blinks, sending fresh tears cascading down his face. "Why are you being nice to me? You don't know me."

My frown eases a little. I brush the droplets from his cheeks. "We haven't known each other long, that is true. But we've had sex twice now, and you're going to be sleeping under my roof for the next couple of nights. I call that intimacy, which is a different kind of knowing you. Does that make sense?"

He shrugs, the gesture somewhat petulant, but I let it slide. He's clearly torn up about this.

"And as for why I'm doing this, it's because it's just the right thing to do. You gave me a gift by offering yourself up to me without question. I broke you down, now I have to put you back together. It's just logical."

By the way he's scowling, I assume that to him it's not that simple. Well, unfortunately for him, this is my house, and these are my rules, and they are non-negotiable.

"Kiki, if you won't let me care for you, I'm afraid I'll have to cut our liaison short. But I really don't want to do that.

Will you please trust that I know what's best and submit to me? I'm not going to hurt you. I would never do that."

He cringes again, feeling so small in my arms. But I am patient, and after several moments, I'm rewarded with a tiny nod. "Good boy," I say firmly, kissing his hair again. "That's my good, pretty doll."

Gently, I encourage him to stand. He sways on his feet, so I'm also up in a flash, hugging him to me. Together, we walk toward the bathroom. The sun is dipping outside, so I flick the light on before sitting him on the closed toilet lid, then I twist the taps on the tub. When I stocked up his living quarters, I purchased toiletries I like so he could smell the way I want. Everything is floral and fruity, so he'll be juicy and sweet for me. I pour bubble bath into the running water, and soon the room smells of roses.

Turning back to him, I help him to stand once again, then begin undressing him. He's only got the belt and dress left on, so it doesn't take long. I drink in his smooth, creamy skin. He's got no tattoos and just a single piercing in one ear where a tear-shaped pearl hangs. He's a blank canvas for me to paint on.

"Beautiful," I say yet again, skimming my fingertips along his stomach and over the curve of his hips. In that moment, there's no hiding that he is definitely a man. Yet I am still attracted to him. I'm relieved. I didn't want to be lusting after an illusion. After all, part of the point of having him stay here was that I can see him whenever I want. Yes, I've told him that I want him to always be beautiful for me, but that doesn't necessarily mean dolled up to the nines.

He's quiet as we wait for the clawed bath to fill. Once I stop the water, I take his hand and help him step inside, then perch on the side and take my time drenching his body with a sponge laden with water and suds. Eventually, his shoulders start to relax. I ask if I can wash his hair, and he agrees.

He also asks me to get his bag of toiletries from his suitcase so he can use a particular product to take his make-up off. I didn't realize how much he was wearing until he removes it.

When I'm satisfied that he's squeaky clean, I help him step out again and then spend a while drying him with a big fluffy towel. I'll be honest, when I offered to tend to him after our scene, I hadn't envisioned that it would be this intense. However, now that we're here I wouldn't change a thing. I meant what I said before. We might only just be getting to know each other, but this kind of intimacy skips a lot of that irritating small talk bullshit.

It's my turn to sit on the toilet lid as I watch him apply several different products to his face that leave him looking plump and glowing. He's wrapped in the towel around his waist to give him a little privacy. I figured he might need it after being so upset. When he's done, he turns and looks at me as I smile back at him. He huffs and fiddles with his fingers.

"I'm sorry for being weird," he mumbles.

I stand and pull him against me for an embrace. "You have nothing to apologize for. Thank you for opening up to me and admitting what was wrong."

We both know he didn't really tell me much. I pieced it together from what little he did let slip, and I'm sure there's something more lurking beneath the surface. But we'll never make any progress unless I bribe him a little with flattery, or at least that's the impression I've gotten so far.

"Thank you, Daddy," he says quietly.

God, I love hearing that.

I rub his back and kiss his now-damp hair. "Would you like to see your presents?" I ask.

He leans back and looks at me in surprise. He's barely shorter than me, even if he is smaller. "Presents?" he asks with hope and excitement in his voice.

I chuckle. "If I'd known it would be that easy to cheer you up, I would have led with that. Come on."

I steer him back into the bedroom until he's standing in front of the closet, which I then open with a flourish. It was empty before, so it was easy for me to hang up all the new pretty garments I ordered.

In the past, I've shopped for sugar babies if I want them to wear something specific for our rendezvous. I've never bought a series of outfits for one person, especially not a man. But it goes to show how times have changed because one of the online lingerie stores that I particularly like had entire ranges for people without breasts and with cocks. I was able to find a few dresses as well, and then accessories were easier. The jewelry is in the drawers of the dressing table. We can look at that later.

Considering Kiki is only here for a couple of days, it was probably overkill, but I don't care. In fact, the idea that he'll take these presents home with him and I'll be able to continue dressing him from afar fills me with a certain possessive satisfaction.

"This is all for me?" he asks in a small voice.

I stand behind him and kiss his neck. "Yes, beautiful. I might be new to the concept of playing with dolls, but from what I understand, dressing them how you want is a big part of that. While you're here, I'd love to see you wearing my gifts. They show me you're mine."

"Yes, Daddy," he says softly.

A raw satisfaction seeps through me like warmth from a fire. "Good boy. I got you this to sleep in." I reach into the closet and remove a hanger that's holding up a pale pink silk negligee.

"Oh, Daddy, it's perfect," he says with a timid excitement. He looks over his shoulder and beams at me. He could be faking his reaction, of course. But I can't help but feel like he really does like it.

With a nod, I slip the scrap of material from the hanger so I can put it back in the closet. "Lift your arms," I say, and he complies immediately. The nightdress glides over his beautiful body, fitting even better than I'd hoped. The towel naturally falls to the floor.

"There we go," I say, satisfied. "Now, are you hungry?"

He shakes his head. "Just sleepy, Daddy."

I'm tempted to put my foot down and insist he eat something. Instead, I decide to make snacks readily available in the kitchen. I have a substantial breakfast planned in any case, having already anticipated that we were going to work up an appetite.

"All right, then," I say, placing my hand on the small of his back and leading him back toward the bed.

I pull off the blanket that did its job and protected the duvet from our mess, push aside some of the throw pillows, then yank back the covers so he can get comfy. As he lays his head down, I sit beside him, pulling him to snuggle against my side.

"There we go," I say, content at last that I've seen to my doll's needs. "I'll stay until you fall asleep, okay, Kiki?"

For a while, I assume he's not going to reply. That's okay, I wasn't expecting him to. In fact, I was pleased that he didn't fight me on it. But then his sleepy voice rises up from my chest.

"Kadence."

"Hmm?"

He looks at me and blinks. "My boy name. It's Kadence."

Something stirs within me. I know his name. Something tells me that this is his real one.

"Kadence," I say, brushing back a curl from his forehead. "That's as beautiful as you are." He gives me a small smile and is about to turn his head back again when I cup the side of his face, encouraging him to keep looking at me. "I'm Rafferty."

For several moments, we hold each other's gazes. Then he nods and snuggles in closer to me.

"Good night, Daddy Rafferty," he says.

CHAPTER 9

Kadence

Where the fuck am I?

I was so dead asleep that when I wake in an unfamiliar bed, my first instinct is panic. Is this a hotel? It's certainly not the Sunken Treasure Motel in Paddle Creek. There's a distinct lake of mermaids, fish, and plastic doubloons.

Then it hits me.

McKenna.

No. *Rafferty.*

I rub my chest as my gaze drifts around the room that's bathed in early morning light. There's a gentleness in the soft pastel colors and twinkling glass of the chandelier. I take a few deep breaths and try to slow my heart rate down. As I massage my sternum, I feel the silky satin and lace trim on the negligee I'm wearing.

Rafferty put it on me. He did a lot for me last night.

This was not a part of the plan.

"Shit," I whisper to myself out loud. What the hell came over me? Deep down, I already know. Another panic attack, like the one I had in front of Logan that started this whole mess.

Except this time no one else saw. No one laughed at me. In fact, Rafferty bullied his way into taking care of me.

And just like that, he's not McKenna to me anymore. That's the name he shares with his fuck boi son. Rafferty was the man who gave me another round of mind-blowing sex last night. But then he gave me something else.

His kindness.

Sickness crawls up inside me. I'm not sure how to handle this. I was prepared for him to be a controlling, heartless jerk who wanted his way the whole time. I told myself that would be fine because he's hot, and I would just suffer through any indignities until I could get the evidence I need. I told myself I was okay whoring myself out for pretty things so long as it brought me closer to my ultimate goal.

But the orgasm was so intense and then the sub-drop frighteningly immediate. Perhaps it was an adrenaline crash? Whatever the case, it left me emotionally defenseless when Rafferty wasn't cruel...he was kind.

I bite my lip as shameful tears fill my eyes again. My sister has been warning me for years that I need some therapy. She says I have too much repressed shit and that it's only a matter of time before it starts to leak out, whether I want it to or not. Is that what these panic attacks are?

Both incidents were different, though. Logan humiliated me and made me feel worthless. Then it was the crying itself in front of others that traumatized me more than anything.

With Rafferty...it was when he *didn't* dehumanize me that I broke down. Wasn't that what I wanted from Logan all along?

Did I cry last night because when I got what I wanted, I felt like I didn't deserve it?

I think back to Stanley. Sure, we'd hug and stuff after sex, but he was clear that he didn't like 'that mushy shit.' I always thought that I didn't want that either, but now I'm not so certain.

Maybe I like being a doll because it means that I don't have any expectations of love or affection. It feels safe. But it freaked me the hell out that Logan would fuck me, then not even acknowledge my existence when we met in public.

Kind of like how my rich conservative parents act like they don't have a son at all, at least not one they can be proud of.

Dear lord, I confuse myself. Perhaps Erika is right, and I really should be talking to a shrink instead of concocting elaborate revenge plots. I mean, she's almost certainly definitely completely right about that. But I'm here now, so I'm not sure how much I can walk it back.

And how ironic is it that the man I've painted as my enemy is the only one who's giving me what I want. Not even that. He's giving me what I need without me even knowing it.

If Jessie's friendship and concern were making me uncomfortable, this is in a different league of its own.

I take some more deep breaths and rub my eyes. This—whatever 'this' is precisely—isn't going to be solved right now, no matter how much I try. I'm only here until tomorrow evening, and despite all these frustrating and confusing emotions swirling around my head, I've still got a mission to accomplish.

Ignoring the seed of doubt that's sprouting in my chest, I make the decision to proceed as planned, and that involves being better than perfect and beautiful at all times. Rafferty gave me a pass last night, thanks to my mortifying meltdown. But we haven't got long together, and I'm determined not to let it happen again.

So I pull the negligee off and fold it under my pillow before getting in the shower. I like the products Rafferty bought for me, so I use those as I make sure every inch of me is scrubbed once more. Then I take my time putting on day serums moisturizers, shimmery lotion, and several hair products. Before I get a chance to worry about going and asking for one, I find a hairdryer in one of the drawers of the dresser. Excellent.

Curls and body sorted, I open up the closet again and allow myself to have a proper inspection of the new clothes. For an older, cis, supposedly straight guy, Rafferty has done an impressive job of spoiling me with some seriously gorgeous threads.

Most of them are the same kind of baby doll design similar to my negligee. But there are also a couple of dresses that wouldn't look out of place on Bridgerton, a kimono, and a voluminous party dress. As I explore further, I also discover a lot of panties, some bralettes, feather boas, and even a faux fur coat. I'm not vegan or anything, but killing an animal purely for an aesthetic reason seems unnecessarily cruel to me, so I'm glad it's fake.

I try not to mark it up as another pro point on Rafferty's imaginary pros and cons list that I'm definitely not keeping in my head.

When I sit down at the dressing table to apply my face, I open up the smaller drawers at the top on a whim. My jaw drops as I realize there are a number of jewelry boxes hidden in there, and I assume they're for me. They're mostly diamonds and pearls, but there's one fancy floral necklace that's made from several different colored gems. It would have been so easy to make a piece like that tacky, but it's extremely elegant. I touch it reverently for a few moments before shutting the box lid and focusing on my look for the day.

Rafferty put up with my shit last night, so I feel like I need to get back in his good books. He might have insisted on the aftercare, but he shouldn't have had to do all that for a fun, no-strings-attached weekend hook-up. So I've picked out a mint-green baby doll dress with long, flared sleeves and opulent feathered trimming. It's a little like the outfit he first met me in, only this one has many layers of silky material, so it isn't see-through.

That's why I'm not bothering with any underwear.

He wanted ready? I'll give him ready.

Plus, I have the perfect green pumps to pair it with. After considering my incredible new jewelry collection, I decide to go with pearls, fastening a string around my neck. I once read somewhere that Coco Chanel loved pearls so much because the light is supposed to reflect off them and make your face look radiant. I'm not sure if that's true or not, but it's the kind of confidence boost I'm looking for right now.

Just doing the base layers of foundation and highlighters and all that takes at least half an hour. I'm becoming increasingly anxious that Rafferty's going to come barging in before I'm ready, but I refuse to rush this part of the process.

I know I'm planning on screwing him over. But he was nice to me last night. He deserves to get what he bargained for, even just for a day. A picture-perfect sex doll.

As I add the last few shimmery touches, I finally relax. My stomach also grumbles, reminding me that I skipped dinner because I was so upset last night. I'm not sure if I'm allowed to simply go down to the kitchen and fix myself something or what.

A knock at the door yanks me from my thoughts.

My head snaps in that direction, and I'm unsure of what I should do for a moment. "Kadence?" Rafferty calls gently through the wood. "Are you in there?"

I open my mouth to reply, but then I remember where I am. *Who* I am.

I'm not Kadence anymore.

Careful not to trip over my own heels, I rush to perch on the side of the bed that I thankfully already remade, complete with all the throw pillows. Facing the direction of the door, I relax my body into my doll pose, letting my gaze drift.

"Yes, Daddy," I say clearly.

The handle turns, and the door slowly swings inward. I might be looking into the middle distance, but I can still see Rafferty's eyebrows shoot up. If he'd been expecting a crumpled boy hiding under the covers, he severely underestimated me.

"Hello, beautiful doll," he says appreciatively, stepping into the room and caressing the side of my face. "Don't you look absolutely perfect in all of Daddy's pretty presents?"

"Yes, Daddy."

He rubs his thumb over my glossy lower lip before pushing it inside my mouth for me to suck. He watches me hungrily for a few seconds before withdrawing it.

"Is Daddy's beautiful Kiki feeling okay this morning?"

I want to tell him that dolls don't have feelings. That I don't want to mention last night ever again. But I also want to play the game more, so I let those thoughts and feelings dissolve, holding on to my doll head space.

"Yes, Daddy."

This time, he feeds me his middle finger, making me get it slick with spit, before he pushes me back, turning me ninety degrees as he does.

"Oh, *good* doll," he says breathlessly as he pushes up my skirts and finds that I'm not wearing any panties underneath. The bed dips as he kneels by my feet, and then…

Apparently, my Daddy hasn't had breakfast yet, either.

He wraps his lips around my cock at the same time his wet finger probes my hole. I'm still not sure what his experience with men is, but he knows enough to sheath his teeth so they don't scratch me.

Lying on my back makes it easier for me to stay lifeless, even if his hot mouth feels exquisite and he's already got his finger inside me up to the knuckle. When he strokes my prostate, I have to grit my teeth to stop myself from screaming. He knows what he's doing to me, though, and he laughs, popping off my dick and wiping his mouth with the back of his hand.

"We're going to keep this dress pretty for now, baby doll. So you're going to come down Daddy's throat whenever it feels good for you."

And with that, he dives back in, slurping on my cock and rubbing my sweet spot like he's attempting to entice a genie from a lamp. I try to make it last. I really do. But ultimately, I'm powerless, and he's got me spurting within thirty seconds.

To his credit, he drinks it all down until I'm softening and sensitive in his mouth. He lets me go with a kiss to my shaft, pulling out his finger gently. Then I feel the mattress bounce as he stands up and moves to the bathroom. I hear the faucet turn on as I assume he washes his hands. Then he's back, giving my intimate areas a gentle wipe-down.

Taking hold of my shoulders, he encourages me to sit back up while he stands in front of me. "Look at Daddy, Kiki doll." I do as he says. "Did you like Daddy's special treat?"

"Yes, Daddy," I tell him sincerely.

He grins, his lips reddened and swollen. I must admit I wasn't expecting that. Stanley never went down on me. That was my job. I think he thought that was too submissive, too feminine for him to lower himself like that. Rafferty looks like he really enjoyed himself.

"Good boy," he says, cupping the side of my face. I've noticed that he only ever called me 'doll' to begin with, but now he seems more accepting that I'm also a boy.

If he really did think he was straight—or had a limited

experience with his bisexuality—that's pretty cool. I did that. Or rather, Kiki did that.

"Are you hungry?" Rafferty asks.

"Yes, Daddy," I answer without hesitation. I won't lie. After another mind-blowing orgasm, I've used up so much energy my stomach is threatening to eat itself and I'm worryingly close to feeling faint.

But...he didn't come. I'm supposed to be the one servicing *him* this weekend. He's the Daddy. His needs are the most important. For a second, I'm frozen, unable to decide what to do. I don't really have the words in my doll vocabulary to convey what I'm feeling, so should I break the scene? If I'm abiding by my own rules, I shouldn't technically move of my own volition. He's supposed to guide me.

I can't leave him hanging. I just can't. His bulge is clearly visible in his pants. He's been so good to me.

"Daddy?" I say simply, tilting my head as I look at him and jerking my stiff arm toward his crotch.

He's quick to loop his fingers around my wrist and ease my arm back down. "Daddy's fine, pretty doll. We can play again later. Daddy enjoyed making his doll happy. Kiki can do the same for Daddy later, hmm?"

Relief washes through me now I've been given clear instructions. "Yes, Daddy," I say with a little more warmth than I'd usually employ in doll mode.

"Good," he says with a nod. "Daddy needs to feed his Kiki doll now. He must be starving." Taking my hands, he carefully pulls me to my feet. He takes a second to straighten my hair and dress as he beams at me. "So perfect," he says with a sigh.

I'm expecting it this time when he places his hand on the small of my back and steers me out of the room. When I woke up earlier, I felt completely undone and unsure. I didn't know where I was, or maybe even *who* I was, certainly not what I was doing.

But now I have a purpose again. I am here to perform a duty. I have a mission.

I have given all my control over to Rafferty, and when the time comes, I'll take that control back, unraveling his world. Logan's world. The McKenna reign is over and I'm going to be the one to take them down.

Except as I make my way down the stairs, I can't help but think again of the differences between my two panic attacks. How the two McKennas had such opposite reactions.

Yes, Rafferty is a bastard millionaire.

But does he really deserve his son's punishment?

Honestly…I'm not so sure anymore.

CHAPTER 10

Rafferty

I have to admit that I wasn't expecting Kadence to be ready and waiting for me like that. I almost thought his bag would be packed and he'd be waiting for me to wake up so I could arrange for my driver to take him home.

Instead, we had more incredible sex.

I can't remember the last time I got my partner off and wasn't even bothered about my own orgasm. It's not like I don't want more—I definitely do. But when I saw pretty Kiki sitting on the bed like he was, I just had to have him.

And then there was the other not insignificant issue. I'd barely touched a cock with my hands before I met Kadence. But in that moment, I swallowed him down without hesitation. I figured it probably wouldn't feel all that different from eating pussy, and in a way, I was right. I'd told more inexperienced girls in the past that they needed to sheath their teeth more, so I knew to do that. The rest was basically sucking and swallowing. I'm sure I have things to learn, but Kadence seemed to enjoy it enough, and he can always give me pointers for next time.

Now he has to eat, though, and I won't take no for an

answer. Last night he required sleep more than anything, and I'm hoping from his performance just now that it's done him the world of good.

Fuck, he's beautiful. I appreciate what make-up can do for a person. My wife was skilled at giving herself lovely looks. But it was quite minimalist. Kadence treats his face like a work of art. No doubt it takes a long time to apply, so he must have risen early to complete his routine by the time I came in to greet him.

I like that he put that effort in for me. I like that despite hitting a road bump last night, he's still invested in us having a good time this weekend and using our limited time wisely.

We only have around thirty-six hours now. It doesn't seem like enough.

Kadence wasn't the only one being productive once he woke up. I'd showered quickly, then made my way downstairs to prepare a decent breakfast. Charleen likes to have kitchen staff when she stays here, but I enjoy cooking for myself. Not only do I find it fun and relaxing, but I also think it's important to continue to do things like that in order to stay humble.

I know I'm rich. I like being rich. But I don't want to become so detached from reality that I forget how to be a real human being.

As Kadence is being Kiki the doll for me, he doesn't give any reaction as we step into the dining room, but I'd like to think he's impressed. I've sliced up and displayed several different kinds of fruits. I might not have made the selection of pastries myself, but I've arranged them on cake stands so they look particularly appetizing. I thought we might take a little time to come back downstairs again, so I'm glad I left the eggs, hash browns, and bacon on heated plates, covered. There's juice and coffee to drink and a couple of different kinds of milk to go with the coffee or cereal if that's what he wants.

He allows me to guide him into the seat I've prepared for him. In a spontaneous splurge, I ordered him some fine china embellished with a soft pink rose pattern. He's got large and small plates as well as a delicate teacup. The glass doesn't match the set exactly, but it's also got rose petals crafted into it.

If Kadence wants to eat as himself, I've got plenty of my regular crockery. But I'm glad I put this set out this morning and that he's in full Kiki mode for me. I'm enjoying playing this game and don't really want it to end. In fact, that's given me an idea.

Once he's settled, I go to my own chair and reposition it so I'm by his side. "Is there anything here that you don't like or are allergic to, Kiki?" I ask him.

"No, Daddy."

"Good," I say with a nod.

I don't explain what I'm doing or justify myself. I simply take his plate and load it up with a little of everything. Then I take the special floral embellished fork from his set, scoop up some scrambled eggs, then hold them up to his lips.

Obediently, he opens his mouth, and I get a rush of satisfaction as he lets me feed him.

"Good doll," I murmur.

Starting with the hot food so it has less time to get cold, I methodically hand-feed my pretty doll bite by bite. I was worried he didn't eat last night, so now I can make sure he gets more than enough. It's a real thrill having someone depend on me so completely.

Once I'm satisfied he's consumed a decent amount of potato, eggs, and meat, I hold a glass of apple and mango juice, mesmerized by how his throat bobs as he swallows half the glass down.

"Do you take your coffee with milk?" I ask him.

"No, Daddy."

"Sugar?"

"Yes, Daddy."

"Just one?"

"Yes, Daddy."

I fix us both a cup. I like mine searing hot, but as he's relying on me, I want to let his cool for a minute. So I take a moment to sip my own drink as my gaze trails over my perfect doll. He sits beautifully still, just waiting for whatever I want to do to him next.

God. It's easy to see how I could quickly become addicted to this. Letting him go tomorrow evening is extremely sensible, even if it doesn't feel like I've had enough time to explore all the things I want to do with him.

When was the last time I was this excited by anyone? By *anything?* I can't say. It's like how I felt as a teenager when I first discovered how to masturbate. Utterly captivated and constantly desperate to slip away so I could get my next fix. I lost a whole blissful summer to my own insatiable appetite that year.

The thought of a whole summer with Kadence flashes before my eyes, but of course that's ridiculous.

Isn't it?

Charleen will be away until August, she said so herself. Logan has his own apartment. He never comes back here unless I summon him. I could keep on a skeleton staff. They're more loyal to me than Charleen in any case. I speak to them like the real people they are. She criticizes anything and everything that isn't precisely to her liking. There would probably be enough people I could trust to keep working while Kadence is around. The rest I'll just give full pay and an extended vacation.

I blink, not sure if I'm seriously considering this or not. Well, I don't have to make a decision right now, do I?

I feed Kiki a few strawberries and slices of melon, swiping drips of juice from his chin. I ate a few bites of hot food before I went up to find him, so I'm not ravenous at the moment. I just sample a little fruit myself, getting more out of feeding my doll than I do eating myself.

After half a croissant, I sense him slowing down a fraction in his chewing.

"Are you getting full, baby doll?" I ask.

"Yes, Daddy," he says.

I smile, feeling smug. "Good boy," I praise him. "You ate so much for Daddy." I take a moment to dust off any crumbs from his face and dress. Impressively, his lip gloss still looks flawless.

I might have to do something about that.

But in a minute. I want to make sure he's finished his breakfast completely.

"Would you like your coffee?" I ask him.

"Yes, Daddy."

I don't want to risk spilling a hot drink on his lap—not to mention ruining his pretty dress—so I place the cup between his fingers and encourage him to drink it himself. As he does, I eat a little more myself. The last thing I want is a rumbling stomach, and it seems a shame for this food to go to waste.

After several minutes of comfortable silence, he pauses with the cup in both hands, hovering in front of his chest. I peer over to see that it's empty, so I carefully take it from his fingers. Having finished eating myself, I wipe my hands and mouth on a napkin, then turn my attention back to my pretty living doll. He's still as I card my fingers through the soft curls at the back of his head. I could pet him all day.

There's nothing stopping me, after all.

I think back to his perfect lip gloss and smirk.

"Is Kiki too full for a little of Daddy's dessert?" I ask. I know we've agreed that he'll do whatever I want, whenever I want. But I don't want to make the poor boy sick.

He doesn't seem concerned though. "No, Daddy," he says with just a hint of excitement, his eyes lighting up the tiniest amount.

I turn in my chair and unzip my pants. "Good boy."

———

It's been a beautifully lazy day. I can't remember the last time I experienced anything like it. Perhaps on vacation in the Bahamas when Logan was young?

Usually, I get easily bored at the weekend, so I find myself logging in to my work accounts just to pass the time. But today, I have company, someone to entertain. After breakfast, I lead Kadence back to his room and tell him to relax. Maybe try on some more clothes for his Daddy. I'm sure it's not good for him to stay in the doll head space for too long, so I really am giving him time to decompress.

It gives me a chance to clear away the mess in the dining room and salvage the food I can for a later meal or snack.

As soon as I'm done, my mind almost wanders to my office. Instead, I take myself to my study. It's not quite big enough to call it a library, but it does have an old-world feeling to it that I enjoy. I've been meaning to rearrange several bookshelves for some months now. Apparently, today's the day.

I'm not sure how long I'm in there before I sense movement at the door. Kadence is wearing a different dress and has applied a different lip gloss after I successfully smeared the last coat everywhere. My cock perks up just thinking about it.

"Are you busy, Daddy?" Kadence asks in a sweet voice. So

he's dolled up, but not a doll. Good. I love playing with him in that mode, but I also want a little company as well if that's not too much to ask.

I shake my head. "I'm just puttering," I say, holding up the book in my hand. "Doing some organizing. Would you like to join me?" I jut my chin at the chaise lounge. "You can look pretty while I work if you like."

He scrunches up his nose as he smiles, then sweeps into the room in a cloud of pink tulle. "Do you like reading?" he asks. He drapes himself on the couch as if he's ready to be painted. I'm not much of an artist, but I must admit the idea of trying to capture his naked form on paper while I sip a glass or two of red wine sounds like a heavenly way to spend an evening.

"I'll read anything and everything," I say, meaning it. I love autobiographies, science fiction epics, historical tomes, and war stories. I've even picked up a couple of Charleen's spicy romance books from time to time. "You?"

"I like crime thrillers," Kadence says without missing a beat. "The kind where detectives hunt down killers. Especially if there's a proper mystery involved."

I raise my eyebrows. It's not fair of me, I'm sure, but I was expecting him to tell me that he does little more than scroll his Instagram feed. Licking my lips, I look around at the piles of chaos I've made since I started pulling volumes down off the shelves. "Ah," I say as my eyes land on the cover I was searching for. "Have you read this? It's one of my favorites."

I offer it over to him, and he leans forward carefully, his hand reaching out like I'm holding a grenade and he needs to check that the pin is still in place. "I don't think so," he says, accepting the book. He studies the cover, nodding approvingly, then flips it over to read the blurb. "It's set in London?"

It's my turn to nod. "The author is British."

"Cool," he comments, taking a minute to finish reading

the text. In that moment, when his face is a little slack in concentration, I can see just how young he is. My heart swells with an urge to protect him.

But he's a man, not a baby. Besides, I couldn't do all that much to help my own son. What makes me think I could do any better with Kadence?

"Have you traveled much?" I ask as I resume my task of reorganizing the books.

Kadence shrugs and gives a sad little laugh. "I made it from home to here if that counts."

"Have you never left the country?" I ask.

He shakes his head, his eyes determinedly on the pages he's flicking through. "Nope," he says, popping the 'P' extra hard. "I don't even have a passport. I'm just a simple doll, you see."

"Maybe I can put you in my carry-on, then," I murmur. "Slip you right by security."

He hums and smiles shyly over the book. "Sounds fun, Daddy."

To my surprise—again—he settles quite happily on the chaise lounge and begins to read my dog-eared novel, totally engrossed by a few pages in. I'm distracted by his presence for a while, but then I also fall back into my task. We spend a couple of quiet, happy hours in the study until I look up and realize my doll has fallen asleep.

My heart aches for him.

Not wanting to analyze the feeling too closely, I wrap up my job, putting the last of the books in their new homes. Then I gently ease the thriller from Kadence's grasp, pleased he doesn't seem to have lost his place. I slip a bookmark between the pages just to make sure and leave the book on the coffee table next to the couch.

Kadence is heavy, but I manage to pick him up in a bridal carry. In his sleepy state, he still wraps his arms around my neck and holds some of his own weight, which makes my job easier.

I relocate us to the living room. Ordinarily, I wouldn't eat in here. But fuck it, I'm on vacation. I ensure my doll is all snuggled against the pillows, and drape a blanket over him. Then I stroll into the kitchen and get us some charcuterie bits to graze on. Me for now, and him for later when he wakes. I also pour some juice, but as it's mid-afternoon and a Saturday, I throw caution to the wind even more and also open up a bottle of light and fruity white wine.

Putting on a movie in the middle of the day reminds me of the days my son was sick as a child. It feels entirely decadent, and I love it. As Kadence is still dozing, I take it upon myself to pick an old action thriller from the nineties where the hero races across the globe to stop nuclear war. It's familiar and comforting. The young man sleeping against me might be *un*familiar, but he certainly is comforting. This whole set-up feels so natural with him.

I wonder at his tiredness. His exhaustion. I wonder what he has going on in his life that he needs to escape into being a doll like he does.

I wonder what I can do to help.

That feels dangerous, however. So I console myself that I'm here, now, and that's good enough for the time being.

Try as I might, I'm finding it difficult to keep my hands to myself. I've got a new toy, after all. I'm excited to play with him.

And who could blame me? My doll really is perfect in every way, just begging for his Daddy to wake him up and have some fun.

The only problem is that he starts to wake up first.

And he's not okay.

CHAPTER 11

Kadence

I REALLY DIDN'T MEAN TO FALL ASLEEP. THERE'S JUST something about this man that makes me drop my guard.

That's dangerous.

I'm aware that at some point we move locations. I moan and try to make myself wake up, but Rafferty shushes me and tells me to go back to sleep. So I do.

I wish I could say that my dreams were peaceful, but I don't think they are. It's like sifting through sand, trying to remember anything, but I know I'm distressed and trying to scream at someone, but no sound is coming out.

"No," I mumble.

"Wake up, pretty doll. You're having a bad dream."

"No," I utter once more, feeling myself fight and frown.

But there's a strong hand on me, running up my bare leg and skimming my tummy. Oh, yeah. I'm not wearing any underwear. I'm with Rafferty. I'm...I'm supposed to be tricking him...

"Shhh, Kiki," he says. His voice is soothing, but there's also something firm and no nonsense about it. I find that comforting. Sometimes, especially when I'm spirally and at my worst, I just want someone to tell me what to *do.*

"Daddy," I whimper. If I were more conscious, I'd probably feel pathetic. But I'm still half-asleep, and all I can really focus on is the touch of his hand and the low rumble of his voice.

"Shh, Kiki," he repeats. "It's okay. Daddy's here. Be a doll. Just be a doll."

That, I can do. I can be Kiki. Kiki doesn't have any cares in the world apart from being perfect for Daddy. Kiki can relax. Daddy will take care of Kiki.

Gradually, I let the tension seep from my body. The bad dreams fade away. I remember that I had them, but not what they were about. Daddy Rafferty massages my hip, thigh, and side, hugging me to him. I realize that the TV is on, playing some old movie. Daddy is watching it. I'm just an accessory, something to comfort him as he relaxes.

I switch off, giving myself over to him and his wishes.

That's when his hand drifts over my stomach, heading south, skimming my inner thighs, casually pushing my legs apart.

"What's your color, Kiki doll?"

"Green, Daddy."

As his hand encircles my cock, I remain limp against his side. I have no say in the matter. It's my honor to be his plaything. I might as well be a fidget spinner. My hardening length is just something to absently occupy his hand.

I feel so free.

Yet again I think about how good he is with my kink despite only just stumbling into it. Except it's a distant, floaty idea that's dancing somewhere in the distance. I don't need to worry about big thoughts right now. Daddy will make all the decisions.

He doesn't acknowledge me now that I've shaken off my

dreams and calmed down. His eyes are on the movie as he strokes my cock. I breathe deeply, not letting myself squirm the way I want to. It helps that Rafferty isn't trying to make me come. But he is keeping me hard.

I'm not sure how long he watches the movie for while he plays with me, but I've leaked enough pre-cum to slick his fingers, which he starts probing my hole with. My cock twitches as he pushes one digit, then two, inside me, stretching me out.

Without a word, he withdraws then pushes me down the length of the couch, so my face is smushed into the pillows and my dress falls down my back, leaving my ass exposed. I hear the click of a cap and the snick of his zipper, then smell more fruity lube. It's the only warning I get before the fat head of his dick is pressing against my entrance.

My head is slightly turned so I can breathe. As he starts to rock into me, the image on the large flatscreen dances at a ninety-degree angle, several feet in front of my eyes. With my gaze unfocused, the colors are just blurs. The voices, music, gunfire, and explosions seem far away.

All I care about is the slow rhythm of my Daddy's cock as he luxuriates in pulsing in and out of me, using my hole to make himself feel amazing. His length strokes my prostate, making my heart race and my skin perspire. The side of my face rubs against the pillow, and I worry about my make-up smearing on the fabric.

Rafferty is rich, he can afford to clean or replace it. And I can reapply if necessary. So I stop worrying.

All I need to care about is the way Rafferty moans as his pace increases. How his fingers dig into my hips, anchoring him as he ravages me. I lie limp, embodying the sex doll I promised him I would be.

As he comes, he gasps and shudders, but otherwise makes no sound. The movie on the TV plays on, the hero saying something to the heroine that just sounds muffled to me. I lie still as Rafferty slowly extracts himself. The sofa dips, and I hear him huff and pull some tissues from a box before zipping his pants back up.

To my surprise, he rolls me gently onto my back. My hole drips with his cum and the lube, but luckily I think my dress catches the worst of the mess. My reddened cock bounces almost painfully against my stomach. With the movie's soundtrack swelling in the background, he leans down and once more takes me into his mouth. My stretched and slippery hole offers little resistance as he pushes two fingers inside me and aggressively massages my prostate.

I do my best to remain inanimate, but my orgasm crashes over me like a tsunami. I gnash my teeth, breathing heavily through my nose as I screw up my eyes, tears leaking down my cheeks. He swallows down every drop I give him, sucking on me gently as I go soft in his mouth until he finally lets me go.

He reaches back for the box of tissues once more, and carefully wipes me down before sitting me upright again and tucking me under his wing, pressed against his side. He pets my hair as the movie credits start to roll.

"Good boy," he murmurs.

I sigh, letting Kiki go as I wiggle my stiff fingers and squirm my aching body against him. "Thank you, Daddy," I whisper.

There's a fair amount of food on the table, not to mention juice and an ice bucket with a wine bottle nestled inside. It's like as soon as I notice the spread, my stomach rumbles.

Without me having to say anything, Rafferty reaches forward and picks up a wooden charcuterie board laden with all kinds of goodies. He rests it on the wide arm of the couch, then begins feeding me bite-sized morsels like he did at breakfast.

No one's *ever* fed me before. I try not to grin too much as I lick his fingers and waggle my eyebrows at him. Now that I'm not in doll mode anymore I can show my appreciation.

"You like that, huh?" he says, clearly amused.

"I love it, Daddy," I say sincerely. "Thank you."

He rubs his thumb against my lower lip. It's salty from the little cubes of cheese, slices of garlicky meat, and plump olives he's been feeding me. I suck it and even though I'm sure neither of us is ready for another round just yet, I still feel the spark of chemistry between us.

The credits finish, and the screen goes back to the home-page, suggesting other movies in the same sort of genre. "Can we watch something else?" I ask hopefully. His TV is almost as large as my whole bed, and I'd quite like to pay attention to something this time.

"Of course, baby doll," he says warmly. "You pick."

He hands me the remote and I don't waste much time selecting a movie I saw once a couple of years ago at the theater. I want something I don't have to give all my attention to but that will still hold my interest somewhat.

Rafferty continues to feed me, and also insists I drink a full glass of juice followed by some water. Only then does he let me have some wine. Full and calm, I snuggle against him under a blanket, enjoying how he plays with my hair.

We're about halfway through the movie when I realize that this is aftercare. He snuck it on me. But that's not even the most disturbing part.

I love it.

For once, I don't feel all over the place. I thought it was normal to be fidgety and emotional after a scene. I'm used to the waves of sadness and shame, accustomed to brushing them off as part of the regular rhythm of sex. I always told myself that I was strong. Other subs might need coddling after scenes, but I didn't.

Maybe I don't. However, I can't deny that this feels really, *really* nice.

I swallow the bite of apple and creamy brie cheese, licking my lips as I think that over. So this is just something Rafferty just does with everyone he sleeps with? Part of me is dying to ask him, but I'm overpowered by the part of me that would rather not know.

I'm aware I'm being a brat, but I'd rather live in ignorance and believe that I'm somehow special. That he doesn't spend a typical Saturday afternoon having sex on the couch and a picnic in front of the TV with just anyone.

I'm also not sure I'm ready to admit that this man is simply kind. It's not an act. He would have slipped up by now, I'm sure. He's considerate and takes charge in a way that puts my needs first, not his own.

I mean, yes—he gave that whole speech about me being here purely to be fucked by him whenever and however he wants. He's definitely living up to that promise. But at the same time, he somehow makes me feel like it's all about me. That I'm his priority. That I really am special.

Despite my earlier train of thought, I'm not sure I can cope with that level of attention. I don't want anyone caring about me.

That means they'll have power over me.

"What are you thinking about, pretty doll?" Rafferty asks me, pulling me from my reverie.

I blink and look up at him. I realize I've zoned out and missed at least ten minutes of the movie. That doesn't matter, but I don't want him knowing that's where my mind was at. I'm already giving so much of my power away to him.

"Just pretty doll thoughts, Daddy," I assure him, snuggling closer to his side.

He scoffs and kisses my forehead. I'm not sure he's totally

convinced, but he doesn't ask anything further, so that's all that really matters.

It's not until I go to the bathroom a little while later that I realize I forgot to check my make-up. Sure enough, it's a little smudged. Nothing comically bad, but by no means perfect. I feel a rush of panic and shame as I hastily try to fix it with my fingers, but then I slowly let my hands drop. Rafferty certainly didn't care all evening. Why should it matter now?

Besides, it's getting close to bedtime, and I'm not going to sleep with all this on. Now that I'm paying attention to it again, my eyes feel crusty enough after that nap earlier.

So I slip away to my bedroom to remove all the products before applying night serums and moisturizers. I get into my nightgown with the matching silk robe and find the fluffy slippers he also bought for me. Then I pad downstairs once more. I'm curious yet again about the rest of the house, but I respect that he doesn't want me poking around in his private rooms.

I'm not sure how much longer he wants to stay up or what else he wants to do. That's up to him. It is our last night together, after all. But at least now whenever he decides it's time to go to bed, I'm comfortable and ready for sleep.

Still pretty, though. Obviously.

"Hello, gorgeous," he says as I come back to the sofa, opening his arms for me, and his eyes trail over my new outfit. Pleased that he's evidently still impressed, I cuddle up next to him, pressing a sweet kiss to his cheek.

"Hello, Daddy."

For a few seconds, he studies my face, his eyes lingering on my lips. Not for the first time I wonder if he's going to kiss me there. I haven't explicitly said he can't, but he seems to inherently know he shouldn't. However, for just a moment I wonder if I actually want him to.

No. That would be crossing a line, and I think we both know it, because he taps my nose with his index finger, smiling and breaking the spell of the moment.

"Beautiful."

We finish watching this second movie, and I try not to yawn but fail. Rafferty chuckles at me.

"I think that's our cue to head to bed. Come on. I'll clear all this in the morning."

I want to protest about being wasteful, but looking down at the coffee table, it turns out that we've eaten almost all of the perishable food. I guess it really won't hurt to leave the mess for now. And if that's what Daddy wants to do, that's what we'll do.

He places his hand on the small of my back in the way that I'm growing to love. As we head upstairs, he flicks off the light switches and sets the alarm. It feels cozy like I've never experienced with anyone else before. Like we're tucking the house into bed.

When we reach my room, he drags me down onto the mattress with hunger in his eyes, soon pulling himself free and pushing inside me once again. But this time I don't fall into doll mode. I look into his eyes as he fucks me slowly and tenderly, drawing the experience out until we both come, clinging to each other as we grunt and cry out.

He showers my body, careful not to wet my face with all my nighttime products already applied, nor my hair, so we don't need to dry it. Then he puts my nightie back on and tucks me in. Luckily, we contained our mess, so there's no need to change the sheets.

In the dim light, he looks down at me for several moments as he caresses the side of my cheek. I bite my lip, not sure what he's thinking. Just as I'm about to say "Daddy?" he smiles and leans down to press his lips to my forehead.

"Good night, my beautiful doll."

"Good night, Daddy," I say as he turns off the light, then closes the door, leaving me in darkness.

My mind is whirling, so I figure it's going to take me forever to fall asleep. But I underestimated how exhausted I am, and soon I'm slipping into unconsciousness.

As I finally succumb, I hope my dreams will be kinder to me tonight.

CHAPTER 12

Rafferty

It took everything I had not to crawl into bed with Kadence last night. Not to fuck—he'd quite worn me out by the time I fell asleep.

I just wanted to hold him.

Luckily, I had enough sense to realize that would be a bad idea as things stood. But as I lie in bed, looking up at the ceiling the next morning, I'm aware that the nature of our deal is already shifting, at least on my end.

I want more. I *need* it.

Puffing out my cheeks, I rub my forehead and wonder if I've officially lost my mind. But there's no denying the fact that I haven't been this relaxed in a very long time.

This happy.

I had a hunch that the sex would be good, and it has. No, it's been spectacular. But I've also enjoyed Kadence's company. Simply watching a movie with him yesterday was deeply rewarding. I like feeding and bathing him. I want to make his nightmares stop.

Is this what it means to really *be* a Daddy? Right now, it

feels like so much more than a name to be called in the heat of a scene. It feels like who I *am* to him.

That's…a lot. Not to mention unexpected. I don't think I can reasonably unravel the way I'm feeling about everything by this evening.

Then I remember that I'm Rafferty fucking McKenna, and I never have to do anything I don't want to.

Well…aside from the fact that I'm trapped in this sham of a loveless marriage. But indulging in this tryst feels like the perfect rebellion against that.

I rub the scruff on my chin and debate shaving. Kadence is putting so much effort into his appearance for me, I should at least try and meet him halfway. But, Jesus Christ, I'm so over always having to play pretend and put on a show for everyone around me. Whether it's at the office or at a function or even around my own damn wife. It was such a novelty wearing a T-shirt and jeans yesterday.

I don't want to be a slob, however, so I still shower and pick out some fresh clothes before heading to Kadence's room and knocking on his door.

When this started out, I had some fantasy of barging in there whenever I damn well felt like and using my doll any way I wanted. But I love that he makes sure to be all made up for me. As much as I enjoy playing, he isn't an inanimate object.

I respect him enough to give him boundaries.

Sure enough, I hear a slight commotion and a panicked squeak. "Just a minute, Daddy!" he cries out a second later.

I chuckle and shake my head, even though there's no one to see me do it. "No rush, pretty doll," I assure him. "I just wanted to advise you to wear something a little sturdier and more covered up than usual. Come down to the kitchen when you're ready."

This time I feel the pause through the door, as if I can see him frowning. "Yes, Daddy," he says eventually.

I could tell him what I have planned, but I enjoy surprising him. Something tells me that not a lot of people have done that in his life, at least not in a good way. In fact, I have a horrible suspicion that he's suffered a fair bit at the hands of others. So I want to put a smile on his face.

Besides, I'm Daddy, and I call the shots.

I wait for him downstairs, sipping coffee and reading an article from the Financial Times on my phone. It's perhaps fifteen minutes before he appears, peering around the corner almost like he's nervous. I grin, seeing that he's picked a perfect outfit.

"Good morning, gorgeous," I say as he slinks into full view.

I was most concerned about his footwear, but he's got on the ankle boots he wore when he arrived. Sneakers would be better, but I doubt he would have bought anything like that if he was planning on being a sexy doll the entire visit. Besides, they'll be fine for what I have in mind, I'm sure.

He's paired them with lace-trimmed socks that just peak over the top, a lilac tennis skirt, a white polo shirt, and a pale pink jacket. Sunglasses hang from the center of his shirt's collar, and his face looks beautifully done up as usual. His curls are fresh and bouncy, and as he steps closer, I smell how he's enveloped in a cloud of sweet candy scents.

"Is this okay?" he asks shyly.

"Flawless," I tell him, resting one hand on his hip and skimming the other up his thigh to cup his ass. Good. He's got decent underwear on. Still lacey panties, but all the important bits appear to be covered.

No one should bother us today, but I don't feel like sharing my doll with anyone. Not right now.

"I made us a picnic for brunch," I tell him, resting my

hand on the wicker hamper that's waiting for us on the countertop. "Are you up for a walk to the creek?"

For a moment, he just stares at the basket. Then he blinks and looks at me. "You want...? Um...okay. I mean—yes, Daddy." He beams at me, but I can see in his eyes that he's still very thrown by my suggestion.

Yep, as I suspected, I doubt he's used to anyone putting much thought into how they treat him. If something as simple as a picnic can floor him like this, it's going to be easy to spoil him. I want to surprise and delight him. This old dog still has some new tricks up his sleeve.

I'd checked the weather forecast earlier, but I always find you never really know the truth until you're out in the elements. Luckily, it's a beautiful day as we walk across the grounds, following the path that cuts around the lawn on the estate where it then follows the edge of the woods until we reach the trickling water. This wide but shallow creek eventually flows down to the nearby town that took its name from it.

I carry the hamper on one side and hold Kadence's hand on the other. He's quiet, but I catch a glimpse of him every couple of minutes as he looks around at the scenery. I wouldn't peg him to be a city boy, but he certainly seems charmed by our surroundings.

"So you can come up here anytime you want?" he asks eventually.

I nod as a warm zephyr caresses our skin. "This is all part of my estate. I have a team that comes out every quarter to make sure nothing gets too overgrown, and there are fences to keep people from trespassing. I've never really had any trouble."

I should say 'we,' but Charleen hardly pays any attention to the grounds, rarely venturing farther than the patio when she hosts people here. It's me who likes to take myself wandering, although I can't recall the last time I did.

It seems that Kadence is inspiring all kinds of changes in me.

We find a shady spot under a tree close to the creek so we can see the glittering water splashing over the pebbles, making faint rainbows with the fine misty spray. I lay out a thick picnic blanket and open up the hamper, revealing that as part of the design there are two plates, cutlery, and short-stemmed Champagne flutes secured to the lid. Kadence's eyebrows rise although he doesn't say anything.

Hey, just because we're outdoors doesn't mean we have to slum it.

I fix him a mimosa, then proceed to open up the various boxes of food I packed this morning. I've chosen sandwiches, crudités with dips, potato chips, and little cakes this time rather than bother trying to prepare anything hot.

As Kadence isn't in what he calls 'doll mode,' I encourage him to help himself. He moans as he takes a bite of a mini cheesesteak roll, his eyelids fluttering shut as crumbs cling to his lip gloss.

Fuck. I want to kiss him so badly. But I know that would be crossing a line that he's silently put into place. Kissing is so intimate. This is supposed to be a fling.

Supposed to be.

I reach into the basket and show him what I'd hidden near the bottom. "I thought we could spend some time out here reading together," I say as I hand him the crime thriller he started yesterday. For myself, I've selected a somewhat trashy-looking navy adventure that I kept telling myself I didn't have time to waste on.

Well, now I do.

His eyes light up. "Oh, yes," he says eagerly, taking it from my fingers with care. "I'll have to see how much I can read before I leave later."

He laughs, but then he gives me a strange look before gulping down some of his drink and taking another bite of his sandwich.

Bingo. Perfect opening.

"About that…"

He shakes his head and hastily swallows. "I was kidding. I can finish it with an eBook."

I laugh softly as I reach over and cup the side of his face. "I want you to finish the book, Kadence."

"But I—"

"I don't want you to leave tonight."

This time, he stares at me for several long seconds, unblinking. "You…huh?"

I brush any crumbs that might be lingering from my fingers, gently extract both the book and the roll from his grip, then slip my hands against his, holding them firmly.

"I'm not a fool," I explain. "I understand that time stops for no one and it's not possible to exist in a bubble. But I would like to discuss a slightly more long-term arrangement."

His eyes search mine for a moment. "H-how long-term?"

I shrug. "At least a week. Maybe two."

Maybe all summer. I don't say that out loud, however, so as not to spook him. This might fizzle out after a few days of trying to navigate real-world obligations. But I want to give us the breathing room to at least *try*.

He nibbles on his lip. "How would that work?"

"Well," I say with a grin. "I would indeed need to work, but I can do a lot of that from home. I can scale back the staff. We'll mostly have the place to ourselves. I'd like you to stay here and keep me company."

He swallows and frowns, his gaze flicking down to the ground before looking at me again. "I can't work from home."

That's not a no. I like that he's thinking this through practically.

"You said you weren't fond of your job," I prompt.

He scoffs. "Oh, I hate it. I just don't know what else to do right now, and I have bills to pay."

Excellent. Time to be exactly the kind of asshole people think I am.

"Quit. Tell them a better offer came along. If you're just temping, I assume you don't have to give any notice."

His jaw drops. "Uh, yeah. I mean, no. No, I don't have a notice period. At least I don't think I do. But I do have rent and—"

Cutting him off, I shake my head. "You'll be doing a summer internship with me. As a personal assistant. I'll set you up with a proper salary. Maybe even send you out to get coffee and do laundry from time to time."

He's still looking shell-shocked at me, so I wink to try and reassure him. He shakes himself like he's coming back to his senses. "You're serious, aren't you?" he asks breathlessly.

I rub my thumb against his cheek, loving how he leans into the touch. "Kadence," I say in all seriousness. "I'm not ready to let you go, yet. I can't promise you anything beyond a few weeks. But I would very much like to explore more of this dynamic. You excite me in a way I've never experienced before. I'm not talking about a relationship or anything public. I'm talking about indulging in you for as long as I desire. If you could tolerate me for a little longer, it would mean a lot to me if you'd consider what I'm offering."

For a minute or two, I watch him breathe. "You'd really pay me to stay here and be pretty for you?"

I can't help but laugh. Trust him to cut to the heart of the issue. "Yes, baby doll. If that's crossing a line for you—"

"I didn't say that," he interrupts hotly. "There's nothing wrong with sex work."

"No, there's not," I agree. I've always had a more liberal attitude toward the world's oldest profession than a lot of my puritanical peers. As if most of the men I know haven't indulged in paid pleasure at least once in their lives. Hypocrites.

"Until you get bored of me?" he clarifies.

I don't mean to sound harsh, but the realist in me knows there is only a short lifespan for an arrangement like this. "Until we wish to part ways," I say diplomatically. "At which point, I'll write a glowing professional reference for you and have my executive assistant sign and swear to it."

Audrey won't mind. I've asked her to do far worse, I'm sure.

I still have one hand cupped against his face and the other is holding one of his. He uses his free one to rub his sternum as he looks out over the grass. Leaves rustle and the creek bubbles, providing a calm background to his decision-making process.

Honestly, it hadn't really crossed my mind what I'd do if he said no. I appreciated he'd most likely think on it, but I was confident he'd say yes. Because I'm certain he wants this as much as I do. And he'd be a fool to turn down the kind of money I'm willing to give him.

My boy isn't a fool.

So when he turns his gaze back my way and gives the smallest of nods, I'm not surprised, but I am extremely glad.

"Good boy," I murmur, brushing my thumb over his cheekbone.

I want to kiss him. God, I want to kiss him.

Instead, I pull him into my lap and make short work of his underwear. We make love in the glorious sunshine, then spend the rest of the day lounging around eating, drinking, fucking, and reading. Kadence finishes his book.

We have time now.

CHAPTER 13

Kadence

WHEN I WAKE UP THE NEXT DAY, I'M YET AGAIN CONFUSED FOR a few seconds by my surroundings. Then it hits me.

I'm still here.

Rubbing sleep from my eyes, I exhale and wonder if this is a terrible mistake or the best decision I've ever made.

Jessie is supportive—enthusiastically so. My texts haven't exactly been giving him all the facts. He still has no idea what drove me here in the first place, and I didn't confess to any of my embarrassing breakdowns. So with the information he has—i.e. that I've extended my weekend visit with my new sugar Daddy—he thinks it's all very romantic.

I'm honestly not sure what's going on.

Financially speaking, it's a no brainer. Rafferty is going to pay me more per week than I was going to make a month at that awful office job. I'm sure I'll start getting bored eventually. However, for now at least, all I have to do for him is be beautiful and let him fuck me whenever he wants. I can do that.

He's also feeding me, buying me more clothes, and letting me have free rein in his study, where he's organized all his books. As long as I put anything back where I find it, I can read whatever I like.

You could call me a whore and you wouldn't be wrong. But how is this much different from being a sugar baby? We're both consenting adults who have agreed to terms we find mutually acceptable. I don't care what the specifics of the law might say, I don't think I'm doing anything illegal.

Morally gray? Scandalous?

Yeah.

Rafferty is creating a paper trail if he's going to put me on his company's payroll. All I'd need to do is get some video footage and…

And the idea makes me feel sick.

The whole point of me coming here was to get my revenge. But I'm starting to think I really can't do this to Rafferty himself. At least not in any way that does him any lasting damage.

Rubbing my chest, I think it over hard. He's been nothing but kind and generous to me. More than that, he's been honest and respectful. The complete opposite of his son. Yes, he wants to keep the relationship secret. It's not like we're dating. And it's not unreasonable for a prolific man to keep a sexual affair on the down-low. Especially when everyone thinks he's straight and married.

But the difference is he's not *ashamed* of me. If anything, by the way he beams at me, I'd say he's proud of me. Which is ridiculous to admit, but that's how I'm feeling. Like he appreciates me. In fact, the way he wants to keep me all to himself *is* kind of romantic. As if I'm a precious jewel he wants to admire in private. There's nothing wrong with that.

No. Rafferty doesn't deserve to be ruined. I don't know what the deal with his wife is, but she's not here, and I am. If he wants to keep that long-distance thing alive for whatever reason, let him. He's earned that much from me. Not to mention how compromising images could end his business. He *definitely* doesn't deserve that.

Logan still deserves his comeuppance, though. The was he treated me was so beyond unacceptable, and he needs a harsh lesson in consequences. So…yeah. Whenever Rafferty decides he's done with me, I'll just take whatever evidence I've collected and go gloat to Logan that I spent however long banging his dad. That ought to humiliate that self-loathing, closeted little homo enough.

Hopefully, Rafferty will never even have to know. I doubt Logan would be brave enough to confront his old man about it. That would involve explaining how we know each other or why Logan would care if we were together.

Happy with my new plan, I release the tension from my chest like a butterfly taking flight. It's time for a shower and to get my game face on.

Who knows what Daddy will have in store for us today?

———

"Kiki?" Rafferty's firm voice rings through the house.

He explained over breakfast that he had back-to-back meetings that afternoon, so I'd have to entertain myself. After I took myself on a walk around a different part of the grounds, I'd settled in the study and started reading another book. Checking the clock on the mantel, I frown. I thought he wouldn't be done for another couple of hours.

Placing a bookmark between the pages, I leave it on the coffee table, rise from the chaise lounge, and hold on to the door frame as I look down the hallway. Sure enough, he's standing at the threshold of his office.

"Yes, Daddy?" I reply.

He simply crooks a finger at me in a 'come hither' gesture, then walks back inside.

Curious, I sashay down the corridor like it's a catwalk. As usual, I'm in a floaty dress and heels with no underwear for easy access. This outfit is a combination of raspberry pink and cream, and I specifically picked a fruity lip gloss to match. Not that Rafferty will be getting a taste, but it makes me feel particularly delicious as I head toward him, my steps echoing off the walls.

Perhaps one of his video conferences got canceled, and he has a little free time. Oh, the things this doll could do for him in just ten minutes.

He's not going to regret offering me this ridiculous deal. No one in their right mind should pay so much for another human being just to relax in their home. I almost feel guilty.

There are several reasons I should feel guilty.

No. This whole thing might have started insincerely, and he doesn't even know that. But I'm going to make it up to him regardless. What he doesn't know won't hurt him. I'll just make sure he never, ever finds out how I've been using him.

Anyway, enough melancholy thoughts. Time for him to use me in a much funner way.

When I enter his office, I find him sitting back down at his desk. He doesn't look up at me, and I can hear a voice coming from his computer. Going with my gut instinct rather than waiting for an instruction, I move closer, peeking at the large monitor as I round the desk.

He's on a video conference. There's got to be twenty faces looking back at him. I'm just out of the frame.

I'm too busy trying to work out what's happening to notice him raise his hand, but suddenly he's yanking me between himself and the desk. I gasp, my eyes going wide as I flick them over the screen.

Nobody's even flinched at my appearance.

That's when I look for Rafferty's display box and see that it's both black and muted.

We can see and hear everyone else, but they can't see or hear us.

Rafferty shoves his chair back, the wheels a low rumble on the wooden floor. That's all the warning I get before he pushes me down, my chest pressing against his desk, my face an inch from his keyboard.

An austere-looking woman is giving a brisk report about some kind of percentages. I don't take in much more than that before Rafferty's hands are pulling my ass cheeks apart, and his tongue is delving between my crack.

Inhaling deeply, I relinquish my control and stop worrying what's happening or what *could* happen. Rafferty's work colleagues have no idea what we're doing right now. But with all their eyes looking our way it certainly feels like they're watching their boss eat me out. He hums and moans as he sucks and licks and probes, his spit dripping down my balls.

Fucking hell.

I stay still for him, ever the obedient doll. But I can't stop my gaze from drifting up and looking at all those unsuspecting faces.

The very first time he fucked me was in public. But they were all strangers, not to mention consensual guests at a big old orgy. These people have no idea what they're being included in—and they never will do, I imagine. But it still feels incredibly *naughty*.

Someone else begins speaking as he moves his face away from my ass. From the extra lube he smears down there and the other squelching noises, it's pretty clear what's going to happen next.

It seems like the oblivious people on the screen are discussing funds from certain projects and whether or not they'd be better off allocating them elsewhere. Everyone who speaks is calm and methodical. Rafferty's desk clatters as he thrusts inside me, lube running down my thighs. He wraps his hand around my neck as he starts pounding me hard and fast.

"Good boy," he grunts. "Feels so good for your Daddy. Pretty doll. Take it. *Take it.*"

"Can we get your thoughts on that, Mr. Rafferty?"

I'm already immobile, but those words send icy panic through me, and I freeze up.

Not Rafferty, though.

He slows his pace before letting my throat go and casually clicking the symbol to unmute himself. For a terrifying second, I think the video is going to start as well, and everyone is going to see either my face, his dick in my ass, or both.

But the picture remains black as Rafferty begins to speak.

"There's nothing further to add on that particular project," he says as his cock slides slowly back, and then he drives it home *hard.* I bite my lip and screw up my eyes, desperately trying not to make a peep. But that bastard continues to torment me, fucking me slowly as he calmly talks to his team. "In fact, the entire town is turning out to be a more frustrating investment than I'd initially anticipated. I'm going to discuss this further with Larry and Jeff, who've done the most work with me on this, but as much as I'm loathed to admit, it might be time to sell off and move on."

There's a murmur of agreement, but his words have actually pulled me out of a perfectly decadent headspace.

The project is a town? One he owns? Is he talking about Paddle Creek? The town that was there for me when I wasn't welcome at home anymore? The place he continues to buy up and leave to languish?

What the fuck?

Anger flashes through me, and for a moment it's very easy for me to remember why I came here in the first place. His lousy son treated me like garbage, and I wanted his whole family to be ruined. Rafferty—the McKennas—didn't become filthy rich by playing by the rules or even by playing nicely.

The urge to open my mouth is suddenly overwhelming. One 'Yes, Daddy, *harder!*' would be all it would take. Twenty of the most senior members of his company would have a difficult time un-hearing that.

I take a breath.

But nothing comes out.

Someone else starts talking. Rafferty leaves his microphone on but bends forward to whisper in my ear. I feel the press of his suit against me, the bite of his belt and zipper against my thighs and ass. I remember what our agreement was that we made yesterday.

His business is none of my business. He's been kind and generous to me. We're here for a fun time. I don't want to betray him. I really don't. I'd regret it if I hurt him like that.

As if proving my point further, he caresses the side of my face as he licks the shell of my ear and speaks in such a low tone, I almost miss his words altogether.

"Such a good, perfect boy for Daddy. Pretty doll. I'm going to come in your ass now with everybody listening. I know you can be so good for me and not make a sound, my perfect doll. Just lie there and take Daddy's big, hungry cock."

"Yes, Daddy," I murmur back.

What follows is almost silent. He's careful not to slap against me, but he drives into me deep and fast. His breathing is controlled, but the way his fingers are digging into my hips tell me how wild he's feeling. My cock is trapped between my stomach and the desk, the material from my dress rubbing against it as he plunders my ass.

As he comes, his body goes rigid as his member pulses, shooting his load inside me. The meeting continues. Rafferty clears his throat and interjects, adding some comment about a deadline as he softens inside me. I breathe slowly and carefully through my nose when I feel like I want to lose it.

When Rafferty's done giving his opinion, he reaches over and mutes himself once more.

I can't help but gasp in relief.

In a whirl, he pulls out of me, drops back into his seat, spins me around, and draws me onto his lap. His seed is dribbling out of my hole and onto his pants, and my leaking, throbbing cock bounces between us, red and angry. He looks directly into my eyes as he wraps a lubricated hand around it, ignoring the people talking on the screen behind me.

"Jesus fucking Christ," he mumbles against my neck as he starts to aggressively jerk me off. "You're so perfect, Kiki. That's one of the hottest fucking things I've ever done in my life. Be noisy for me. Tell Daddy you love him. Come. Scream. Be Daddy's good boy."

Like he's flipped a switch, I let go of all my restraint, no longer clinging to my doll state. My head drops back as I wail and thrust into his slippery hand. My climax is building like a tidal wave, but I cling to it, wanting it to grow bigger and bigger until it's all-consuming.

"Yes, Daddy, yes!" I howl over the voices coming from the computer. "So good. I love it. I love you, Daddy. Make me come all over you. Like that. Yes, Daddy. Fuck. *Yes!*"

As I start to spurt all over his expensive suit, he sucks and bites my neck, marking me like an animal. "Who do you belong to?" he growls against my skin.

"You, Daddy," I cry, tears spilling down my face as I continue to shoot thick, creamy ropes. He milks me until my balls are totally empty and I'm shaking against him, twitching as he continues to play with my over-sensitive cock.

"Mine," he snarls, sucking again on the same spot on my neck. "Daddy's perfect little doll."

The meeting trundles on behind me, the words a distance drone. I cling to my Daddy, our soft cocks rubbing together, our mess smeared all over our clothes.

I gasp, my face still wet with tears, too many emotions tumbling through my brain.

This is a mess, and I don't mean the sweaty, cum-stained state of us.

When did this no-strings-revenge-plot become so complicated? Because I have a feeling that as it stands, I am so far beyond the point of no return.

What am I even doing anymore?

And how am I going to walk away and forget that any of this ever happened?

CHAPTER 14

Rafferty

I THINK BOTH KADENCE AND I ARE A BIT SHELL-SHOCKED after the stunt we pulled during my meeting. There's no denying what an electrifying thrill it was, but it was also far beyond anything we'd done before, and there were a lot of emotions on both sides as we came down from the high.

Thankfully, we didn't have to wait long before the conference call came to an end. I stripped us of our soiled clothes to deal with later, then led Kadence to the bathroom where I cleaned him up and wrapped us both in fluffy robes. Placing a gentle kiss on the spot I sucked raw, I grip his shoulders before looking into his eyes.

"I would like you to be as comfortable as you like for the remainder of the evening," I tell him, holding his eye contact so I can read whether or not my words sink in. "If that means sweatpants and one of those weird sticky masks on your face, that's absolutely okay with me."

That gets a small giggle out of him, and I'm glad. I'm certain he was into the sex. It was borderline non-consensual for my staff, but as far as I'm concerned, what they don't know can't harm them. I'm almost certain Kadence was just as into it as I was.

Still…

"Is everything all right?" I ask, rubbing my thumbs against his shoulders through the robe.

He blinks at me. "Hm?"

I lick my lips and study his face. "Did you need to safe-word back then?" I kick myself. We talked about non-verbal signals, but I did tell him he had to be quiet. Was *that* a step too far?

Before I can spiral, he vehemently shakes his head. "What? No? Rafferty, that was seriously hot."

I exhale and nod. "Okay, good. But…is there something else?"

He nibbles his lower lip and looks away from me. So that's a yes. But before I can probe him further, he turns back to me with that dazzling smile of his. "I'm just tuckered out from all this incredible sex," he says, fluttering his long lashes at me. "A quiet self-care night sounds divine, actually."

I'm not sure I entirely believe him. However, I don't really want to prod too hard against whatever his sore spot is.

After all, there are things I'm not admitting to him, let alone myself.

"You go get comfortable," I say, rubbing his arms.

I can't stop myself from reaching up and playing with one of his curls, casually touching his face as I do so. I love that I get to do that still. I love that he's still here.

"I still have some work to finish off, but then I can perhaps make us some pasta."

He nods. "I am very here for carbohydrates," he says solemnly. "Especially if they're covered in cream or cheese or both."

I laugh, feeling a bit lighter. "Carbonara it is, then," I say.

I send him on his way, then head to my bedroom to

freshen up and pull on some sweats of my own, also keen for comfort. My eyes drift to look at my bed as I change. The bed I share with a wife I haven't loved for years and probably never even loved in the first place.

The past three mornings I've woken up wishing Kadence was beside me. *Missing* him almost, even though he's never even set foot in this room.

What's going through his head? Is he having thoughts like that? I know we made our agreement pretty damn clear, but I can't help but wonder…I can't help but *yearn* for a little more.

Maybe a lot more.

It's a phase. It'll pass. I'm just mad with lust and the energy of a new infatuation. The novelty will wear off soon enough, and I'll be extremely grateful that I didn't do anything drastic like burn down my life for him.

For the next week—couple of weeks—couple of months —who knows?—the point is that we can indulge in this bubble. It's a fantasy that will no doubt stay with me for the rest of my days. I'll always look back on my summer fling with the beautiful boy who made me lose my senses.

For now, he's mine to play with as I please. To tend to as I wish. My doll isn't just here for me to fuck. He's a living, breathing pet for me to dote on. He's not going to fight me when I want to fuss over him and spoil him. In fact, he's lapping up every moment of it.

Everybody wins. Nobody gets hurt. Charleen will never have to know, and actually, I'm sure she'll be grateful when I return to my public husbandly duties with a renewed enthusiasm come the fall. She'll have no idea that she'll be indebted to a kinky young man, but I'll know.

I'll always know. I'll never forget.

Shaking my head, I pull my old, faded Harvard hoodie on and refuse to dwell on the matter any longer tonight. This is why I asked Kadence to stay on, why I'm paying him. The only deadline here is when I realize the tryst has reached its natural conclusion. Or when Charleen announces she's coming home. There's no point in dwelling on how I'll feel when Kadence leaves my life for good, not when he's here right now.

I've got time to make the most of him.

And if tonight that's playing make believe as a regular couple just having dinner and watching TV or reading books together, then that's what we'll do.

Because I'm Daddy, and I can pander to whatever whims I might have, even vanilla ones.

If I want to imagine just for one evening what life might be like if Kadence and I were actually dating…well, that's between me, myself, and I. No one else ever needs to know.

Not even Kadence.

———

The next couple of days bleed into each other. Kadence and I fall into something of a routine. We don't risk another escapade during any of my meetings, but we squeeze in plenty of time for fun activities nonetheless. He's always beautiful for me, and I enjoy fussing over him.

But I know he's not telling me everything, and whatever it is, it's simmering just below the surface.

Does he want to call it off? Was the sex at my desk too much? Is he bored already? I have to say that I'm very much enjoying the domesticity of having him here all the time. I thought he was happy taking time to read and walk, and I've heard him filming so I assume he has a TikTok or whatever. I trust him to be discreet as that's an essential part of our deal, so that's not my concern. I don't believe he's stuck for things to do. But I can't really think what's plaguing him other than restlessness.

He is half my age. Perhaps it was foolish to think he'd be seriously interested in me. If he's just here for the money, that's fine. But I don't want to feel that way when we're together. In fact, I'm paying him for a service, and if I'm not getting it, then I can call the whole deal off right now.

Unfortunately, a frustrating meeting with a company I'm supposed to be moving an acquisition forward with leaves me in a bit of a temper. So when Kadence is quiet during dinner, I finally snap.

"I do believe that when you came to stay with me that we made it clear one of my rules was that you had to be upfront with me."

His eyes go wide before he looks left and right. "Um… yeah? Is there…what are you talking about?"

I place my knife and fork down on my plate before lacing my fingers together and inhaling slowly through my nose, counting down from five so I don't snap any further and say anything I'll regret.

"You have something troubling you that you refuse to discuss. I'm not saying you have to disclose every thought that crosses your mind. But when it affects your behavior when we're together, it becomes my problem."

He blinks at me before something dark flashes across his eyes. "It's nothing," he says stiffly. "Or I mean, it's my problem, and I'll do better at letting it go."

"Not good enough," I say. "If something is wrong, you need to let me fix it. Our time together is supposed to be an escape. I know we're playing roles, but I specifically don't want any bullshit when that's what the rest of my life is filled with."

He scoffs at me, folds his arms over his chest and leans back in his chair. Our dinner has been abandoned on both our plates. I know my appetite has vanished. I'll be extremely disappointed if this is already the end of our arrangement.

However, there is a part of me that's impressed that he's not afraid to stand his ground with me. He's not shying away or crumbling. But he's also still holding out, and I'd like to know why.

Right now.

"Fine," he cries eventually, throwing his hands up. "I know I'm supposed to just be a doll for you to play with, and the last thing you want is any kind of *business* advice from someone who only just graduated college, for fuck's sake. But you want to know what's on my mind? I'll tell you."

It's my turn to blink in confusion. I caught the part where he was perhaps having trouble with the boundaries of our relationship. That I can sympathize with. Him moving in and us spending all this time together is bound to fuck with our heads, no matter how no-strings we wanted to keep this.

But he's got opinions on my *company?*

"Go on, then," I say with a jut of my chin.

He swallows and scowls at me for another few seconds. "Paddle Creek is my home," he says in a low voice. "I left my parents behind because they're from a shockingly elitist community of rich bastards like you who think they can just bully their way through any situation. They did not want a gay son, so they were not going to have a gay son. I either stayed and lied or moved and lived. I chose Paddle Creek because despite being a dump, it's actually super fucking queer-friendly."

"Right," I say when he pauses, not quite following.

"Nothing works there because of *you.* All those businesses are closed down or run down because of *you.* You're playing some sort of long game with the real estate and it's choking the whole town. Now you just want to sell it off and forget like you didn't ruin everything for a whole decade or more?

These are people's lives we're talking about! Not pieces on a Monopoly board! I know you're not used to being a minority and will probably spend the rest of your life in the closet, but *I won't do that.* Paddle Creek is where I belong now, and it's a queer community. I hate that you don't care about it, and I hate even more how much I care that you don't care because I'm just supposed to be a fucking *doll* for you!"

My jaw is hanging open. His fists are clenched as he slowly gets to his feet, tears brimming in his eyes. "Kadence...I..."

He shakes his head and the tears fall. "I told you that you didn't want to know," he rasps, avoiding my eyes. "I told you it wasn't any of my business. If you want me to leave, I understand. Just...give me a minute to calm down, okay? I don't...I never meant to...this is too much..."

I'm unable to think of anything to say as he marches out of the dining room. But my head is spinning as I try and break down the essential points of what he just yelled at me.

He's mad at the way I've treated his home. That's fair enough. My current strategy has been failing, and I've been considering the easy way out.

I realize he must have overheard that information *while I was fucking him,* which is kind of messed up. I need to give him more credit. He's really not just a pretty face, he's got an active mind behind those beautiful ocean-blue eyes.

I knew he lived in Paddle Creek, but his words about why it's his home and how important it is to him send chills down my spine. He's right. I don't know anything beyond the extreme privilege of being a straight, rich, white man. I don't know what it's like to be exiled from my family. In fact—the entire reason I'm trapped in a loveless marriage is because I'm too afraid to rock the boat. I guess I haven't had much of a reason to before now.

But Kadence is correct. I could probably choose to

remain hidden in the closet about whatever my sexuality is for the rest of my days.

He doesn't have that luxury.

He's braver than I'll probably ever be.

It's ironic that his kink is pretending to be a lifeless doll because he's actually the most authentic person in my life right now by a long shot.

And that brings us to the final thing he admitted. He cares. Like I care. He cares too much. It's getting complicated.

The fact that I'm realizing this should be enough to send klaxons off in my brain. Instead, I actually feel relieved that we're on the same page.

Except he said he'd understand if I want him to leave.

Absolutely fucking not.

He's damn straight that he has no right to criticize my business practice. Especially when he has the audacity to be spot on the nose with his observations. But he definitely doesn't get to tell me how I feel or when I should relinquish him from our deal. That's *my* choice. If he wants to leave, that's different. But he's not telling me how I feel.

I've spent too many decades with a spouse already doing just that.

No, we're not done with this discussion, and that little brat needs to understand that he's going to have to try a *lot* harder if he wants to scare me off.

Time to go find him and spank some sense into that perfect butt of his.

CHAPTER 15
Kadence

GOOD GOD. HOW DID I GO FROM TRYING TO CONVINCE MYSELF that I don't care how this man lives his life to climbing up on my soap box and giving him an earful? I'm so done. All I can hope is that he pays me for the time I've spent so far here and gives me a referral like he promised so I can get another job quick enough to not miss paying any bills.

I rub my chest as I storm through the house. I feel like a cat that lashed out with their claws and then exposed their belly.

I told him too much. I never meant to whine about being a sad little rich boy whose parents never loved him. That's not who I am. I am more than their rejection.

I never meant to take a dig at the fact that he's discovering a new part of his sexuality, and I certainly didn't want to point out how precarious the queer situation is in my town—or any town. All it takes is one group with pitchforks to run us out if they want to. It almost happened last year, for crying out loud.

And I should never, *ever* have confessed that I care too much about him. We made an agreement. He told me upfront that this is not and will never be a relationship. Why does it bother me so much that he's a heartless bastard? Hello? Millionaire? I always knew he couldn't be this rich without stepping on people.

I don't have the right to want better from him.

Right now, though, I feel like the power imbalance has spiraled wildly out of hand. He's always been in control, but at least it was on my terms.

Without being entirely aware of what I'm doing, I find myself stomping past my room on the second floor, venturing farther into the house than I ever have before. Farther than I'm supposed to be. But I just have to go, to walk, to push, to…

Slowly, I stop by a door that's ajar. From what I can see, it's another bedroom.

Rafferty's bedroom. It's got to be.

Feeling reckless, I step closer and ease the door open. Yes. It smells like him. I see his Harvard hoodie draped over an armchair.

I shouldn't be in here. But a savage part of me doesn't care. He pushed and I broke, exposing myself like a frightened animal in the wild, begging for mercy from a predator.

Now it's his turn.

I don't really know what I expect to find in here, but just stepping over the threshold feels like a rebellion in itself.

The silk bedsheets are cool to my touch as I silently make my way around the room. It's about twice the size of mine, so it's not entirely surprising that there are two chandeliers hanging from the ceiling. There are so many closets and chests of drawers it makes me wonder how much clothing his wife brought with her and how much is still left here. Several large potted plants sit on the wooden floor, their foliage complementing the same sage green paint on the walls that I saw in the entrance hall and corridors. A thick rug lies under the enormous four poster bed. The view from the balcony is spectacular, looking out over the grounds for miles and miles. The whole place screams opulence.

And it's all fake.

Aside from the Harvard sweater, I don't see any of Rafferty's fiery personality in here. There are no photos, no artwork, no collections of knick-knacks or whatever else you're supposed to have in the room in which you sleep. It's all so neat and tidy and...

What's that?

There's something folded up on the nightstand closest to me. It looks like tattered paper that should be in the trash. I know I shouldn't, but it's so out of place I just have to step closer and pick it up and...

My heart skips a beat. Nothing in this room is messy or personal or passionate, as far as I can see.

But Rafferty McKenna has the napkin I wrote my number on by his bedside.

My skin prickles with heat and then chills. My throat tightens. My hands shake. It doesn't mean anything. It doesn't.

It *can't.*

Telling myself that doesn't stop my heart from racing, though.

I don't know how long I stare at the damn thing, but when I look up, I realize I'm no longer alone.

Rafferty is in the doorway, his legs apart, his fists clenched. Despite working from home, he's still wearing pants, a shirt, and a tie, making it that much easier for me to feel the power radiating off him.

I almost flinch. But I catch myself in time, gritting my teeth and letting the napkin drop back on the nightstand like I couldn't care less.

"You shouldn't be in here," Rafferty growls.

I swallow, giving myself a second to think. "If you want me to leave, I understand—"

"Stop talking," he snarls as he storms into the room, reaching me in less than half a dozen strides. He grabs my face with both his hands, and I gasp in shock. He's shaking. He stares into my eyes, his lips inches from mine… "You belong to *me*," he says. "I decide when I've had enough of you, and I'm not done with you by a long shot, Kiki doll. Do you think I'm angry because you talked back to me? I *want* your honesty."

"Then why *are* you so angry?" I taunt him, half hoping he'll admit that this is fucking him up as much as it is me.

He keeps saying he wants authenticity, but who are we really fooling here if not ourselves?

For a second, I genuinely think he's going to kiss me. But instead, he shoves me down onto the mattress and crawls on top of me, only pausing on his knees to rip his zipper down and pull out his hardening cock.

"I told you to stop talking," he hisses as he moves farther up the bed, hovering menacingly above me as he pins my shoulder down with one hand, then feeds me his red, dripping dick with the other. "Bad doll," he mutters as I moan around his length, my hands falling on either side of my head as he takes his hurt and rage out on me in the best way he knows how.

I take his cock willingly, sucking him down. I don't want to think about feelings. I don't want to examine why I want this man's good opinion or why I want to respect him so much. This entire situation has been messed up from the start, and perhaps the only honesty between us at all has been when we're fucking.

He uses my mouth roughly until he suddenly pulls back, leaving me gasping for air and spluttering, spit and precum dribbling down my chin. He's already shoving up my dress and ripping my panties down my legs. I guess it shows that he was right—the fact that I wasn't scampering around commando perhaps proves that my attitude shifted. I didn't want to be so readily available for him.

I am now.

He doesn't waste any time taking both our straining, leaking cocks in hand, jerking us off together. His breathing is harsh as he looms over me, his eyes blazing. I bite my lip as my heart pounds in my chest.

"Yes, Daddy," I whisper.

He groans, his eyelids fluttering closed. "Who do you belong to?"

"You, Daddy."

"Who's in charge?"

"You, Daddy."

His eyes fly open again. "Exactly. So you're not going anywhere until I say you can, understood?"

"Yes, Daddy," I whimper.

I can feel my climax building, but I'm determined to hold it off until he says I can come. Also…I'm afraid of how relieved I am that he doesn't want me to leave. I'm not ready to go…not just yet.

"You're mine, you bad, beautiful little doll. Just Daddy's. I'm supposed to take care of you, no one else. I've got you, Kiki. I'm here. Come…come for Daddy…"

I'm squealing and thrashing as I let go and start spurting all over myself. He joins me almost immediately as we make a mess all over his huge, fancy bed, shuddering and panting as we ride out our combined orgasms.

I'm still blinking my eyes back open when he collects me in his arms, hugging me tightly to him. We roll onto our sides, and I tuck my face against his neck, hugging him back.

"I'm sorry," he utters into my hair.

I freeze. Now who's showing their belly and hoping not to get savaged? What the hell do I do with this?

Before I can overthink it, I throw my leg over him and dig my fingers into his skin, clinging to him like a life raft. "I'm sorry, too."

I don't know how long we lie there, but eventually, Rafferty lets me go. Without saying a word, he takes me to his en suite, another room I hadn't seen before now. He strips us down and we shower tenderly. Still without talking, he dries us off and wraps us in the fluffy robes he seems to have spare in every bathroom. We walk down the corridor, heading for my room.

I expect him to put me to bed. Instead, he sits me on the toilet seat of my own bathroom and perches himself on the side of the bath. Then he narrows his eyes at my many jars and tubes I have lined up under the mirror.

He wants to help me with my nighttime regime.

Wordlessly—and ignoring the lump in my throat—I point at the one I need first, the make-up remover. What follows next is a sort of charming, clumsy, but affectionate face painting session. He doesn't stop until my skin is plump and glowing.

Then he does finally lead me to the bed, retrieving my nightie from under my pillow. He pushes my robe down my shoulders, letting it pool on the floor, then pulls the negligee over my head.

He strips the duvet back so I can climb between the sheets before tucking me in and stroking my hair back.

"Good night, my beautiful doll," he says warmly.

"Good night, Daddy," I whisper back.

When he closes the door and I'm left in the dark, the floodgates open. I'm not sure why I'm sobbing so hard, but I don't fight it. I just let every sad, lonely, nasty thing I've been bottling up break free until I've got nothing left.

Luckily, there's a box of tissues on my nightstand, so I can clean myself up. I take deep, shuddery breaths, then a long drink of water from the glass Rafferty always makes sure is there.

I'm exhausted, and my brain feels like mashed potatoes. Good. I've done more than enough thinking today. Tomorrow I can start all over and reassess what a complete cluster-fuck this situation probably is. Right now, I just need sleep, and lots of it.

Plenty of time to screw everything up again in the morning.

CHAPTER 16

Rafferty

IT WAS PERHAPS TOO EARLY TO PUT KADENCE TO BED, BUT I know how exhausted I am and figure it would do us both good to have some space for the night.

I take some time clearing the dining room table. We didn't eat as much as I would have liked—especially Kadence—so I'll be sure and make up for that in the morning. I'd been easing off the big breakfasts as we settled into a more regular routine, but tomorrow I feel like I might make us omelets and sausages.

For now, though, I scrape the plates clean and load the dishwasher. Then I pour myself a measure of whiskey and go to sit out in the quiet nighttime of the patio.

So much for this being a simple sex-fueled affair. I should have known better. But I've never tried to pursue anything longer than one night with anyone since I got married. I foolishly thought I had this under control.

Nothing could be further from the truth.

God, I'm such a fucking cliché. Is this a mid-life crisis? Is that what's happening right now? I'm risking my marriage and my business for a young man—a *man*—I only met less than two weeks ago?

There are some hard facts I need to face, though. And funnily enough, I'm starting to see they don't necessarily involve Kadence, even if he's inspiring me right now.

This sham with Charleen has to end. I don't know if I want to come out—and I'm certainly not thinking of committing to anything with Kadence. But being with him has really shown me how trapped and unhappy I am. I'd rather be divorced and free to fuck any tasty minx I want than continue lying like we are.

And as for my company…trust my spicy little doll to say what no one on my board has had the guts to. I have dropped the ball when it comes to Paddle Creek. I've been listless, drifting. Sticking to a plan I made over a decade ago and now trying to abandon ship rather than fix all the damage I've caused.

When was the last time I truly built anything? I make investments all the time, but I've gotten so used to delegating all the details. I saw Paddle Creek as an easy coup—I wanted to sweep in and buy it out from under people's noses so I could reimagine it in my own image and make something bigger and better than Albertson.

All I've done is let people down. Stifled them. Choked them.

Perhaps it would be easier to sell it on to someone who could start over. But I'm beginning to feel quite strongly that this is my mess, and I need to fix it. That actually the idea of doing a one-eighty excites me.

I can invest capital from other ventures. I don't need to sell off the real estate I own at a premium, especially as Kadence is right. The town does have a reputation as being down on its luck. Why am I waiting to raze it all to the ground when I could just be expanding on what's already there?

We don't need another Albertson to appeal to straight, white, married couples with kids. Paddle Creek is exactly what it always has been and what it always should be. Eccentric. Bold. Audacious. It should be a queer haven and a tourist attraction.

In other words, exactly the kind of low-brow investment my board is going to hate.

They've always been one hundred percent behind my long-term goal of gentrifying the area. I've told them I'm basically giving up and going to sell what we've got for a profit. If I do this, I'll be lucky if they don't riot.

Tough. I'm the boss. I'm the Daddy. And I've got a hot young thing asleep in my house who's talking the most sense I've heard in years.

We don't need more of the same. We need to celebrate being different. Because *I'm* different, and there's no point in denying it any further.

This pretty doll, this kinky little brat, has rocked my world in more ways than I can count. So if this is some sort of mental breakdown…so be it. I'm done with the bullshit. I've been saying so for a long time now. Perhaps this is the catalyst I needed to start living that authentic life I've been yearning for.

But I don't have to make any big decisions right now. Tonight, I can just sip my whiskey and watch the stars. In the morning, Kadence and I will try again.

We've still got time.

———

By the third time I knock on the door, I start to get worried. "Kadence?" I call through the wood. Still nothing.

I promised myself that I would respect his boundaries, and despite saying on the first day that he better be prepared for me to barge in here and fuck him whenever I feel like it, that's not how our arrangement has worked out at all.

His lack of response is sending a chill down my spine. I thought we were okay after our blow-up last night. But could he have slipped out in the night without me noticing? I feel like I would have noticed. However, I'm not omnipotent.

"Kadence, please let me in," I try one last time. When he doesn't respond, I decide that it's my duty to check on him.

Pushing my way through the opened door into his room…I pause. My heart flips in my chest.

My boy is adorable.

He's asleep in a tangle of bedsheets, his curls sticking in all directions, his nightie slipping down his shoulder. I lick my lips and take in the peaceful tableau, feeling incredibly lucky that I'm privileged enough to get to see such an intimate sight.

He stirs, and I inhale sharply. I didn't mean to be a creep and spy on him while he was sleeping. "You didn't answer," I say as he blinks sleepily at me. "I'm so sorry. I was concerned."

More blinking, then a frown. "Oh, no," he says, his voice rough. "I didn't set my alarm. I'm so sorry, Rafferty. I'll get ready right now. You weren't mean to see this. I—"

"Hey, hey," I interrupt, going to sit by his side. I rest my hand on his bare shoulder, his skin warm against mine. "You don't have to go anywhere, sleepy head. My only concern was your well-being. I didn't mean to intrude."

He's still frowning. "But…that's not the deal. I'm always supposed to be perfect for you."

There goes my heart again, doing somersaults. "You're perfect right now," I assure him. "I think we might have to change the rules a little if you're going to stay here longer.

When it was just a couple of days, it seemed fun to have you be a doll all the time. But I don't want Kiki every waking moment. I want Kadence as well."

While he's staring at me, I take the opportunity to cup my hand against the side of his face and rub my thumb against his cheekbone.

"What's the new rule, then?" he asks uncertainly.

I chuckle softly. "Be Kiki whenever you want. But you're allowed to be comfortable as Kadence, too. We can talk about it, or you can decide. I just want you to be happy."

He bites his lip. "So you really don't want me to leave?" he asks quietly.

As I hug him to me, he tucks his face against my neck, and I rub his back. "I want you to stay as long as we're both having fun. For as long as this is working for us."

I know that's a pretty terrible answer, but I can't admit to him that I don't have all the answers. I just know that right now, everything in me is screaming that he has to stay. I need him by my side.

He doesn't answer me for a few moments, but then he nods against me. I sigh and hold him a little tighter.

"Can we just stay here for a while?" he asks.

Even though he can't see it, I grin and stroke his hair. "I'd love that," I admit truthfully. "Let's just take it easy, then I'll make us breakfast whenever you're ready."

"Don't you have meetings?" he asks.

I shrug. "Nothing important."

That's not entirely accurate, but after three decades of always putting the company first, they can deal with me taking a bit of a back seat for a few days. Especially while I work on dropping the bombshell on them regarding Paddle Creek.

I rearrange us so I'm sitting with my back against the pillows and headboard. Then I pull Kadence so he's snuggled against me, drape the covers over my legs and his body, and rest his head on my chest.

"Why don't you go back to sleep for a while, pretty doll."

He fiddles with the material of my Henley. "You're not mad about last night?" he asks. In that moment, he sounds so young and vulnerable.

Lifting his hand, I kiss the backs of his fingers. "I'm extremely glad you were honest with me," I tell him. "I listened to what you had to say, I promise. And if you don't want to leave, then I would very much like you to stay for as long as possible."

He exhales, his cheeks puffing out. "Okay, Daddy," he says eventually, his words soft and fragile.

"Good boy," I say, satisfied that the matter is closed.

When people get up in each other's business this much and this fast, there's bound to be friction. In fact, it would be incongruous if we didn't butt heads or have opinions about things.

It just goes to show that what we have is *real*. And that's what I wanted all along.

There might be a countdown looming over our heads, but for the time we do have together, I'm glad that it's genuine. I'm showing Kadence Hughes parts of myself I've never shown anyone before. We're sharing something deep and raw.

Whether he's Kadence or Kiki, I wouldn't want to be spending my time this summer with anyone else. I'll treasure every moment we can steal together.

As he drifts off in my arms, I refuse to think about how it's going to feel when he's gone.

CHAPTER 17

Kadence

THINGS CALM DOWN AGAIN OVER THE NEXT FEW DAYS. AFTER my outburst, Rafferty is clearly seeing me and our relationship in a new light. I'm not sure exactly what that is, but it feels less…fraught. I don't know how else to explain it.

I think knowing that he wants to keep me around longer has taken the pressure off. Especially after he came into my room the other morning and clarified that he actually doesn't want a perfect illusion twenty-four seven.

He wants me.

And I'm deceiving him.

In other ways, there's a different kind of pressure, and it's getting worse because it's all on me. Rafferty has no idea that I've been manipulating him from the start. That my intention all along was to humiliate him and his good-for-nothing son.

But he's nothing like Logan. And this stopped being a game quite some time ago.

I try my best not to think about it. Nothing irreversible has happened yet, after all. I haven't even taken any photos or videos. Yes, I know the truth, and when I remember what's really going on, it's getting to the point where it just sickens me.

So I do my best not to dwell on it. I read, I walk, I take naps, and I post on socials. If I didn't have this sword of Damocles hanging over my head, it would be the most epic vacation I've ever had in my life.

When I get really down, I remind myself that Rafferty need *never* know if I don't tell him. I'm aware that getting revenge on Logan was important to me, but when the time comes, I can just decide to do nothing. This can simply be our little secret. It was only ever meant to be a fling, and if that's going to be for a few weeks or the whole summer instead of a weekend, then that makes me lucky. Perhaps this doesn't have to be revenge. It can just be something for me.

It's not as if I've had a lot of luxuries in my life that didn't come from my rotten parents. Maybe I'm owed a little bit of good fortune and happiness.

It seems unlikely, but I can pretend for a while.

That's another thorny, complicated thought I keep having. What we're sharing is *important* to Rafferty. It's not like he's rushing out to buy a bisexual flag for the next Pride parade, but he's certainly had a pretty massive revelation about himself.

Thanks to me.

My intentions might have been nefarious, but his attraction has been real. I know sexuality evolves. However, I think this revelation has been quite out of the blue to him. If I hadn't had this vendetta and pursued him without pause, he might never have realized he could be this strongly attracted to a man.

I can't help but be a little proud of that, even if the circumstances are less than ideal.

"We're going out tonight."

I look up from the chaise lounge that I've come to think

of as mine. Rafferty's leaning against the doorframe of the study with a smirk on his face.

"We are?" I say as I slide my bookmark into place.

He nods and licks his lips. "We're going to a party."

It's clear he doesn't mean for cocktails and dancing.

My heartbeat picks up as I stand. "Is that right, Daddy?" He nods again. "What shall I wear?"

He reaches out for my hand, and I let him take it. "Let's go get you dressed, hmm? I want to make sure you look absolutely divine when I show you off."

Although the majority of the clothes I've been wearing were ones bought by him and he's made quite a few suggestions since I arrived, this is the first time he's actually come and dressed me. I relax and feel like a real doll as he stands me in front of the closet. For a while, he peruses what's on the hangers as well as in the drawers, obviously taking his time in making up his mind.

I don't ask when the party starts or where it is or anything. That's not my concern. These things usually start late anyway, and it's only early evening still. We'll get there whenever Rafferty wants to. I sink deeper into my relaxed state, comforted by the fact that I don't have to take care of anything.

Normally, I'm meticulous about what I wear out in public. However, knowing that everything in this room is exquisite makes it easier to trust that the man knows what he's doing. Or at least will have the good sense to try a few different items to see which works best.

Ultimately, though, he goes for very little clothing at all.

The skirt he slips over my hips has a thick elastic red waistband threaded with gold. Many layers of red silk fall down to my feet, which he's put in delicate gold heels. He places strings of pearls around my neck and wrists and matches them with my own favorite pearl earring. Finally, he pours a shimmering lotion into his hands that he rubs all over my naked torso and arms. I glimmer like a Christmas ornament and feel like some kind of genie that's been released from his bottle.

He washes his hands before coming back to me. "Perfect," Rafferty murmurs, gently rubbing his thumb against my lower lip. "Would you like to do anything different with your make-up, pretty doll?"

"Yes, Daddy," I say without hesitation. If we're going out, there's no way my regular day face will be good enough.

He smiles warmly and places his hand on my lower back to guide me toward my dressing table. Then he sits on the end of the bed to watch me, but I don't feel rushed. In fact, I preen under his watchful eye as he drinks me in.

Luckily, I had a good neutral base look on today, so it's easy enough for me to update with lots of gold sparkles and hints of dramatic red around my eyes. I add some false eyelashes and a strong crimson gloss that I plan to mess up soon enough, and in no time at all, we're good to go.

I thrum with excitement the entire drive there. Rafferty called his chauffeur, so he's in the back seat with me. We don't talk much, but the quiet is actually pretty soothing. Especially as Rafferty has his hand under my skirt and between my legs, idly caressing my inner thigh as he looks out the window.

Of course I don't have any underwear on. Where would the fun be in that?

I expected another house party like Jason and Markus's, and I'm not disappointed. This place doesn't have the seclusion of their home, but it's still a huge mansion that makes my jaw drop as we approach. From the number of cars outside, I'd guess it's already well attended, but a smaller affair than when Rafferty and I met.

The car stops, but Rafferty doesn't get out right away.

Instead, he turns to me, removing his hand from my leg and then touching my chin gently. My heart skips a beat.

"Are you ready to play, Kiki?" he asks directly.

"Yes, Daddy," I say breathlessly.

"You remember your colors?"

"Yes, Daddy."

"And?" He raises his eyebrows. "How do you feel now?"

"Green, Daddy," I say, putting it mildly.

It's not like I've forgotten that our first scene was very public. I'm sure Rafferty trusted those people to be discreet, and if this party is more intimate, that suggests an even tighter circle. But the fact remains that he wants to be seen with me. He wants to play with me...and I assume with others.

In a way, because this is his decision to come out like this, it takes the sting out of anything I was ever planning to do to him. I won't have the chance to make anything scandalous as this is already public to a certain extent. True, it's different from his wife or the board of his company knowing, but it's not a complete secret either. That first encounter could have been brushed off as a wild frenzy of passion.

A repeat is deliberate.

It's a relief. Not that I wanted to humiliate him for a long time now. But it's like he's put the safety catch on and I'm being let off the hook for any responsibility.

I feel free.

And that's before we embark on any mind-blowing sex.

"Good boy," Rafferty says, his eyes roaming over my face like I'm a marvel. "Are you ready to go have some fun?"

"Yes, Daddy," I say.

Our driver opens the door for us, and I slide out first, followed by Rafferty. He keeps his hand on the small of my back as we approach the front door and are let inside. There are people milling around the entranceway, and I try not to act too smug as several heads turn our way.

Yes, I'm stunning. But it's actually a different kind of satisfaction knowing that I'm not here for myself this time.

I'm here to be Rafferty's.

We take our time wandering through the house. There's a bar set up in the living room, and Rafferty gets us both glasses of sparkling apple juice. He ensured we had a decent meal before we left as well as plenty of water. We both know I'll need to be hydrated for what's in store, even if I'm fuzzy on the details.

Rafferty probably doesn't have a plan. I get the feeling he's going to go with the flow and see what opportunities present themselves.

We're not short on inspiration. Plenty of people are already in the thick of it, with lots of partially clothed or just fully naked people finding pleasure in all kinds of ways. It doesn't take long at all for me to feel fully aroused, especially with Rafferty's hand still glued to my lower back.

It also becomes obvious very quickly that he's brought me to an all-male event. Those are the norm, so it's not like I'm uncomfortable. It's just interesting how much I was thinking about the previous party being gender-inclusive when I arrived there. Usually, I'd have to psych myself up to come to an event like this and prepare for any backlash.

But Rafferty is here by my side, literally touching me in a clearly possessive way. Being visibly his helps me to relax. It's unfortunate to admit, but the simple truth is that guys will treat me better because I belong to such a hot, manly Daddy.

It's in that moment I realize the implications of him choosing to come to a party like this. If it was mixed gender, he could brush off his attendance and say he was interested in the women. Coming to an entirely male space is a huge step for him on whatever sexuality journey he's going through.

This is a big deal for both of us, and I can't help but love that we're sharing the experience together.

"What do you like?" he murmurs in my ear, looking around the room.

"Everything," I reply truthfully.

Seeing people get horny makes me horny. I'm a pretty simple creature like that. It's probably why I like being a doll so much and letting people do whatever they want to me. It isn't really about what they do. It's just that they're doing it at all.

I sense his pause and glance over my shoulder to see him licking his lips. "Would you ever fuck a pretty girl for me?" he asks.

I do consider his question for a moment. "Yes, Daddy," I say eventually. "For you, yes."

"You'd enjoy that?" he clarifies.

I half shrug. "I'd enjoy *your* enjoyment, yes. I'm always going to be attracted to men first and foremost, but I can still appreciate a woman. Although, I'd prefer it if I could still be a doll and she was riding me."

His eyes go wide, and it proves my point. His excitement titillates me. I think we're both a bit surprised by my answer, however. I mean, I've known I was gay since I found out what that word meant. The only struggle I ever faced was being painfully aware of how my parents made it clear that it might be an acceptable lifestyle for cheap ruffians, but it would never be allowed within our family.

Internally, I always knew exactly who I was and was never ashamed.

So I've never really considered having sex with a woman before. In that moment, though, I realize it would be no different to whatever—or *whoever*—Rafferty has in mind tonight. If he wants to share me, I'll still be pleasuring him. Kiki doesn't really care how she gets used like that. In fact… pushing my boundaries somehow feels even more in tune with the way my kink excites me. Like it's almost verging on humiliation. I am nothing but Rafferty's sex toy, and he can do with me as he pleases.

More to the point…I *trust* him to do it. That he won't go too far.

That, unlike his son, he'll still respect me afterward. Actually, he might respect me even more. Like me more. Want me more.

I give myself a mental shake. That is way too many thoughts to be rattling around my head. I came here to make everything go quiet. I want to lose myself with my Daddy in physical pleasure. I want to do anything he desires. He owns me. I left all my responsibilities back home.

Back at Rafferty's home, I mean.

Nodding, he looks around the room once more. I can tell he's pleased by the tiny smile that's playing at the corner of his mouth. It's not much, but I like to think I can read him pretty well by now. When he wants me to, of course. There are times when he's a total brick wall, and that's okay if he needs that privacy.

I'll take what little insights I can get.

"Not tonight," he assures me, referring to his desire to see me get fucked by a young lady. That's pretty much a given, considering our company. "But maybe another time."

It's ridiculous how pleased I am by the thought of 'another time.' This may just be a fling, but I don't think the end is in sight quite yet.

To be honest, it is a relief that he's taking that particular card off the table right now. It would be a big step for me to have sex with a woman, and he's already experiencing so many new things already. I want to ask if this is his first party with someone. Stanley and I did a number of public scenes. I think back to my and Rafferty's first night, but that was different. We were strangers then. Now we care about each other, no matter how much we're trying to deny it.

It's not the sex that causes jealousy, in my experience. Sometimes with Stanley it would be fine, and we'd have a lot of fun. But there were times when he made me feel like shit...like when he wandered off or just flat out ignored me.

It was the *lack* of jealousy on his part that was the problem. I can see that now.

Suddenly, I worry I've gotten in over my head. I'm confused within myself about what I want. I'm okay to be passed around, but I want my Daddy to still want me. Is that fair? Are we there yet in our 'relationship'? We're not a couple, after all. What if Rafferty sees another pretty boy he likes and wants to go off and fuck him, leaving me alone? How's that going to make me feel? What if...?

"Hey, hey," Rafferty murmurs in my ear, pulling me closer. "Kadence. What's wrong? Do you need to leave?"

"I...uh..."

I look around, feeling like an idiot. Fuck. How can I really have been so mad at Logan for not understanding my needs? Don't get me wrong. He was still a dick.

But I'm a mess.

Panic is clawing up my throat. However, Rafferty gently presses a kiss to my cheek, and it shocks me into gasping for air.

"Sweet boy," he says softly. "Talk to me."

For a minute, I just breathe. We're by a wall, so enough out of the way not to be disturbed by anyone or really be noticed at all. After several deep breaths, the dizziness subsides. I'm ashamed that I cling to him, but I've been vulnerable so many times in front of him by this point. What's one more humiliation?

"Just…just don't leave me alone," I say. That's it, that's all I need. I don't want to spoil any of his fun. But we came here together, and I don't want to feel abandoned.

His eyes go wide, and he flicks them back and forth over my face. "Of course I'm not going to leave you alone," he says in a firm voice that sends a shiver over my exposed flesh. "You're *mine*, Kiki doll. I was hoping we could play with some other people, but if you need some privacy, you'll have it. I'm also equally comfortable bending you over the nearest piece of furniture and showing all these strangers *exactly* who you belong to."

My jaw drops, and my mouth goes dry, and he fixes me with a challenging stare. Like he's almost daring me to tell him that I'm not his or that he doesn't want me.

His words have jumbled up in my brain, and I'm not quite sure how to respond. "Y-yes, Daddy," I tell him shakily.

His expression softens, and he cups the side of my face. "Yes, what, Kiki?"

I take another deep breath and repeat his words. "Yes, I'm yours, Daddy. We can play however you want. I just want to play together."

He swallows as his gaze blazes into mine. "Good boy. I'm really proud of you for telling Daddy what you need, Kiki. I have no interest in leaving you to pursue anyone else. In fact, for tonight at least, the only person I want to fuck is my beautiful boy. If Kiki would enjoy being played with by some other men and pretty boys, I'd like to see how much you can take. I want to watch you be used, knowing that you belong to me and I control your pleasure. Your body is mine. I want to pass you around, knowing that it's *me* who gets to take you home and *only* me."

He licks his lips, having barely blinked the entire time he was speaking. He's studying me for every single tiny reaction, I can just feel it. As a doll, I don't emote at all if I can manage it. But I'm not quite there yet.

"What color does that make you feel?" he asks.

"Green," I utter immediately. My body is vibrating, and my breathing is shallow. He gets it. He *gets* it.

It doesn't matter what I do with whom because it will actually all be for him. My body is his to use however he likes, *so long as he's there.* My enjoyment comes from knowing he's being turned on. By the power he holds over me.

So long as he doesn't cross over the line and abuse that power.

I feel my throat getting thick and my eyes stinging. As vulnerable as I've been with him, I don't want to cross that line either. I definitely don't want anyone else here to see me crying. But his deep, nuanced understanding of how I tick has unlocked something inside me.

"I love you, Daddy," I say.

It's one of Kiki's pull-string phrases. It's not real. But it goes some way to conveying how I'm feeling right now.

Rafferty opens and closes his mouth once before speaking. "So perfect," he says, stroking my hair. I wonder if he also wanted to say something else but didn't have the best words right now. "Okay. Do you need some time? Or shall we find a space to get settled and see if anyone catches our eye?"

I can't help but adore the way he puts that. As if we're a team with a unified goal rather than him being the one in charge and making all the calls. It makes me feel the opposite of abandoned.

"I'm ready to play, Daddy," I assure him.

He gently caresses my cheekbone with his thumb. He knows not to rub too hard and smudge my make-up because he's amazing.

"Let's go get comfortable, then. Daddy wants to show his perfect Kiki doll off."

I can already feel myself relaxing and slipping away into a light and fuzzy headspace as he leads me by the hand through the house. I get the feeling he might be parading me around, but I keep my gaze unfocused, like a walking sex doll would. So I feel more than see the looks we get, my skin tingling at the attention. But Rafferty's grip is firm and grounding.

After a while, he lowers himself into a plush armchair, pulling me to sit between his open legs, my back leaning against his chest. His stiff cock presses through his clothes against my lower back, where his hand usually sits. He also pulls my legs apart, then he positions my rigid arms at ninety-degree angles and turns my head slightly up and to the left, presenting me to show that I'm not moving. That I'm just an inanimate object, available for others to come and enjoy.

The final step in his preparation is to flick my skirt up and reveal my hard cock, which he wraps his hand around. He rubs his thumb over the slit, encouraging clear precum to bead at the top and leak out.

He kisses my neck, but I don't shiver. I'm just a doll now. I won't move unless he positions me. I won't speak until he expects me to.

"You look so fucking beautiful," he hisses against my ear as he strokes me. "Every single man here wants you. But *I* get to decide who plays with my toy. *I'm* the one who gets to take you home and play with you whenever I want, however I want."

"Yes, Daddy," I say tonelessly, fanning his ego. He's getting off on his power over me just as much as I am submitting to his will. His touch makes me want to scream, but I breathe slowly and evenly, sinking farther into my head space.

My gaze is settled on a painting on the opposite wall. But I can't miss when a twink who looks a little older than me skips up, a bear of a man leisurely strolling behind him. They're both completely naked, and I can feel the energy that binds them together. They're at least here together, if not a well-established couple.

"Good evening, sir," the boy says with a mischievous grin. He drops to his knees and clasps his hands together under his chin. "That's a very pretty doll you're playing with there. My Master said it was okay for me to ask if you're sharing it."

The use of the word 'it' sends makes me want to tremble. I'm just plastic and synthetic hair. I run on batteries. I was made for just one purpose.

To make others feel good.

"Aren't you polite," Rafferty marvels fondly. He's still casually playing with my dick, keeping me rock hard. I feel him look up at the older, bigger man. "What would you and your boy like to do to my doll?"

Suddenly, the bear reaches down and grabs the twink's jaw. "This little slut is a champion cocksucker. It's all he's good for. I want to watch him guzzle down that pretty thing's cream while I fuck his whore hole."

The twink giggles as the bear releases his face. He looks up at the gruff man with adoration. "Yes, Master. I'm so sorry. I just love being fucked so much, and I'm so *very* good at it."

The bear sneers at him. "You're nothing but a cum bucket who needs filling."

"I'm sorry," the twink apologizes breathlessly, his tone still cheerful and polite. "I just love you so much, Master."

"Stop talking and fill that mouth with this toy's cock, now," the bear says. I catch him looking at Rafferty, giving him a nod.

Asking permission.

This couple's vibe is so different from what Rafferty and I have, and it's not exactly what I'm into. But being drawn into their scene is extremely hot and it hasn't even started yet.

Presumably Rafferty nods back because the next thing I know, he lets me go and the twink launches himself at me, sucking down my cock like his life depends on it.

Dear lord, he's good. He moans as his master yanks his hips up so he's kneeling rather than sitting. They've obviously already prepped as he pushes his chubby cock inside him without hesitation and starts fucking him aggressively.

"Take it," he grunts. "Take it, you fucking trash!"

Rafferty wraps his hand around my throat, his breath tickling my ear.

"God, you look amazing," he whispers so only I can hear. "You love that, don't you? That boy knows how to take care of my toy. He's playing so nicely with him."

"Yes, Daddy," I utter.

It would be so easy to chase the high and come quickly, but I know without being told that's not what anybody wants. I have to wait for permission. This is just the start of the show. I have to pace myself.

As it turns out, though, the bear master isn't interested in taking his time. He pants and grunts as he fucks his boy hard, gnashing his teeth before he juts his chin at Rafferty.

"Tell that pretty doll to fill this good-for-nothing whore with everything he's got."

Rafferty strokes my cheek. "Come for Daddy, Kiki. I know you can do it. You're perfect. You do everything Daddy says."

I try not to blink as I stop fighting and blow my load. The twink doesn't even choke, swallowing every drop like a pro. He's gasping and grinning as he pulls off, winking at me and Rafferty as his master comes in his ass with a roar.

Rafferty gently traces his fingers up and down my arm,

giving the other two men time to collect themselves. The bear reaches down and grabs the twink's face again. But this time he pulls him into a filthy kiss.

"I love you," he grunts.

"I know, Master," the twink says happily.

The bear nods at us, and my heart swells. He doesn't say anything, but it feels like he's thanking us. He's telling me that I did good.

As they drift away, I don't need to guess what Rafferty's thinking because he's back to murmuring in my ear. "You were magnificent, Kiki. Daddy loved watching that boy play with your cock. He was so good at it, so hot. You loved it, didn't you?"

"Yes, Daddy," I croak, desperately trying to keep my cool.

This is already so much better than any party Stanley and I ever went to. This is completely the opposite of abandoning me. I feel like Rafferty McKenna and I are fusing together and becoming one being.

The next man who comes to us is a muscular gym rat who asks what Rafferty wants him to do to his doll. Rafferty gets me to move around so my head is in his lap. I expect him to make me suck his cock. But he just strokes my hair and tells me I'm beautiful while the gym rat takes his time eating me out and stretching me with his tongue. Then he fucks me. With a condom, of course, but it still leaves lube and spit dripping down my balls and thighs.

Rafferty asks me my color. I'm floating in a dream, but I tell him green. More men flock to us. He asks me my color after each one fucks me. When two of them want to double-team me, Rafferty is the one to reposition my tired, aching limbs so I can ride one of them while his buddy also penetrates me from behind.

Rafferty watches us, his hand resting just above the bulge in his pants. He hasn't touched himself once.

But he's ready for me now. I'm ready for him.

Unable to physically take much more, when he asks this time, I tell him my color is yellow, and he immediately wraps me in his arms.

"You were so incredibly perfect, Kadence," he says, holding a bottle to my lips and gently tipping cooling water down my throat. The use of my other name helps Kiki fade away. I want to be present now with Rafferty. I want to talk to my Daddy as he coddles me and tells me that I'm gorgeous and hot and better than he ever could have imagined.

I feel more like myself than I ever have before. This complicated kink of mine—the way I have to juggle my needs in my regular life and in scenes—doesn't seem so complicated anymore. Not with Rafferty. I've never felt so cherished and wanted in my life.

I don't care if this is just a summer fling. I don't care if he never comes out of the closet. For now, this thing we have… it's real.

Without speaking, I paw at his zipper. He understands, and within moments he has it open and shoves everything down so I can straddle his lap and ease his gloriously unsheathed length inside my well-stretched hole.

Everything those other men did was all just for my Daddy's pleasure. Everything was only for him. I wrap my arms around his neck, just enough strength in me for one last ride.

I undulate slowly, and he meets every thrust. Our eyes don't waver from each other. I stare into his soul as we move like the waves crashing on the shore.

"I love you, Daddy," I whisper again.

But this time I lean down and kiss him on the mouth to prove that it's really true.

CHAPTER 18

Rafferty

I COME WITH KADENCE'S SOFT, CHERRY-SWEET LIPS STILL ON mine. He shudders and sighs, spurting only a little after everything he's done tonight, then pretty much passes out in my arms.

Holy. Fuck.

I'm still reeling from finally coming after sporting a rock-hard erection for god knows how long. This has been, without a doubt the most thrilling erotic experience of my life.

And then the bastard kissed me.

My heart is racing a mile a minute as I tuck his face against my neck, stroking his damp hair as I soften inside him. This 'I love you' felt different from all the others in a way I can't quite describe. But I was acutely aware of how we hadn't kissed before. How much that felt like a hard limit.

Will Kadence regret it in the morning? Was he just over-stimulated and exhausted?

Or did he really mean it?

There's no way to know that until I can talk to him, and

even then, I won't push. He initiated the kiss. I'll give him the room to tell me what that means.

Until then, I've got Daddying to do.

It's immensely satisfying to be the one who's completely responsible for my boy's well-being. Those other men might have fucked him, but only because I wanted them to.

He's mine to protect now.

I chuckle when he grumbles as I gently extract myself and switch our positions so he's the one sitting in the armchair now. Within seconds I clean myself up and tuck everything away. It would feel undignified to me to walk around naked like a lot of these other men are doing. To each their own, but I'm aware of what makes me feel good, and that's when I'm in charge and have all the power.

Kadence curls up, and I carefully wipe him down. He mumbles sleepily, cuddling a throw pillow, and my heart fucking melts.

Where did this perfect young man come from? It's like someone created him especially for me when I didn't even know what I wanted, what I *needed.* He excites me in ways I never could have imagined, but he also pushes me to challenge myself. Thanks to him, I'm thinking outside the box in so many areas of my life, not just my sexuality.

He makes me understand the possibilities are endless.

I hate to wake him, but there's no way I can carry him when he's out cold, no matter how much I might want to. I need a little help—and if that doesn't feel like a metaphor for my whole life, I'm not sure what will. However, I do take his heeled shoes off so he's steadier on his feet, and wrap my arm securely wrapped around his waist.

"Come on, good boy," I tell him as we start walking toward the front door. "You can do it for Daddy. We're going home now."

He smiles at me like he's punch drunk. Now he's taken his

shoes off, he's the same height as me again. He taps my nose, looking at me through thick eyelashes on heavy lids. "Home," he repeats.

I know it's not really *his* home. But I can't deny that the place feels more alive to me with him living there than it has in years.

Luckily, the driveway is paved rather than stoned, so he can walk to the car I've recalled without having to put his shoes on. Once I've bundled him into the back seat and got his belt on, I tell the driver to head home and immediately put up the partition window. I've barely got my own belt on before Kadence snuggles up to me and falls back asleep.

I cling to him the entire way home.

When we arrive, he wakes with a little more clarity, and I'm able to get him inside the house on his own two feet. I walk him to his room, my heart fluttering in my chest as we reach the threshold.

"I have to take my make-up off," he groans, rolling his eyes. "I'm going to pass out again the second my head hits the pillow." He pauses before reaching out to touch my chest, his fingertips blazing hot through the thin material of my shirt. "Thank you for tonight, Daddy. It was perfect."

"You're perfect," I automatically respond, wrapping my hand around his and holding it close. "My perfect Kiki doll. Thank *you.*"

We stare at each other for a moment that stretches into two. Then three. I open my mouth, not sure what I'm going to say.

Kadence slips his hand free with a sweet smile. "Good night, Rafferty," he says warmly.

It's not a rejection. It's a boundary. One we both need. I nod and give him just as warm a smile, full of my appreciation. He really was spectacular for me this evening. And he did himself proud by articulating what he desperately wanted.

Something I suspect he hasn't always received in the past.

Care.

"Good night, Kadence," I tell him. "I'll see you in the morning."

I step away rather than waiting to watch him close the door in my face. I glance over my shoulder just as it clicks shut.

My bed feels emptier than ever that night. Part of me winces with guilt at the thought as technically this is Charleen's bed as well. But *technically,* she's living in another world in California and doesn't really have any say in who keeps me warm.

I think she loves that guy. Why won't she just admit it, file for divorce, and go *be happy?* She could go build a life with him on the West Coast. It's not as if Logan needs us around much anymore. He hasn't for quite some time now. She already does her job remotely, so what's the big deal?

The court of public opinion, I guess.

She doesn't want the stigma of separating our two families, and truly believes it will negatively impact our business. I'm sure the company would be just fine. But am I sure enough to gamble it and pull the plug on this farce?

There would be no going back from that.

Of course this hasn't really been an issue up until this point. I was content not to rock the boat and simply carry on with the arrangement as it was. But now…

Now.

Now there's Kadence.

I punch my pillow, flip it over to the cool side, then sigh as I lay my head back down. Here, in the dark of night there is no escaping the truth of my thoughts. I'm fully aware that this was supposed to be some fun at a party, then a debaucherous weekend, then a summer fling. I've treated the fact that it will have to end at some point relatively soon as just that: a fact.

But why?

I have no loyalty to a marriage that's been dead for years. We're not doing anything illegal.

I'm being held hostage by my own fears.

Logically, I am fully aware that there's nothing wrong with being gay or bi or whatever it is I am. I know it doesn't matter that I'm old enough to be Kadence's father. He's an adult, and so am I. We're both of sound mind. It doesn't matter that we're kinky—I'm sure a lot of people are as well in their private lives. That never needs to become public knowledge.

But deep inside, am I worried that my board will look down on me if I announce I'm dating someone who's not only much younger than me but also male? 'Worse' than that —he's not simply male, either. He's complex. He wears beautiful make-up and isn't afraid to don a dress or a skirt.

There are at least a dozen men I know in my professional circle who would rip him to absolute shreds for those things.

The realization dawns on me that I'm not just afraid of any potential consequences for myself.

I want to protect Kadence.

Puffing out my cheeks, I exhale long and hard. Now that makes much more sense. I haven't ever been a coward, not once in my whole life. Calculated before taking any risk, yes. But the fear churning in my gut hasn't been for me all along.

I don't want any of those phony socialite vultures coming for my boy and picking his choices and values apart like an autopsy. It's painfully obvious to me how desperately he's trying to find himself right now, not to mention that he's still clearly moving past some previous trauma. He was just looking for a good time. He doesn't deserve to have his life ruined.

So does that rule out a future for us? I mull over that kiss again in my mind, my hand rising almost subconsciously to touch my fingers to my lips.

Is it possible that Kadence sees a future for us in any shape or form?

I'm aware I'm reading a lot into a single damn kiss, but I can't help but feel like it's changed everything. That the last 'I love you' changed *everything*.

There are too many factors I'm uncertain about. Would Kadence be interested in dating or going public? Or is he enjoying this because it's all clandestine? Secrets are alluring. Would the mundane, everyday existence as a couple interest him in the slightest?

Although…isn't that exactly what we've been doing these past couple of weeks? Our time together hasn't felt like a vacation. Don't get me wrong, it's been incredibly exciting. But I've also been working. He's been pursuing his own interests. I'd be happier if he had a career he was passionate about, but the idea that I could give him the room to discover what that is in time is appealing to me.

Is what we have just a glimpse of how life could actually be?

Groaning, I rub the heels of my hands against my eyes. Nothing is getting resolved until I speak with Kadence and gauge how he's feeling. He could very well wake up and regret the kiss entirely. He could regret the whole *night*.

Somehow, I doubt it. I know what I saw. But it feels too dangerous to get my hopes up.

No. The only thing I can do is what I've been doing this entire time. I need to lay down my wishes without any bull-shit. Give him all the facts. Then he can make up his mind as to where he stands and what he wants. If he still wants to take his money and part ways…I think that might really give me an understanding of what people say when their heart is breaking.

Hell, who am I trying to bullshit now? I'd be fucking devastated.

But if he wanted to stay…to try being a real couple…well, we wouldn't have to do everything all at once. It's not like I'd have to hold a press conference about coming out of the closet or introducing him to the world. Perhaps I could just quietly and calmly inform Charleen that we both know that this marriage is over, and I'll be starting divorce proceedings. It won't screw either of us, after all. We'll both still be filthy rich.

The main difference is we'll also both be free.

I respect the woman. She is my partner and the mother of my child. I want her to be fulfilled and content just as much as I want those things for myself.

But above all else, I want Kadence.

Who knows if he really is just my exciting new toy and the shine will dull in time. All I know is right now, I need him. I refuse to let him go.

Tomorrow, I'll find out how he feels about that. Yes, I will still wait for him to start the dialogue. But you better believe that I will be leaving the door open for him and giving him all the encouragement. He can think about how he feels, but my emotions are going to be laid out with nothing to hide.

Because I'm not afraid of him.

Or I should say I'm not afraid of being *vulnerable* with him, which is an entirely new experience for me in my own home.

I'm terrified that he'll want to leave.

But if he stays, it's going to be because I know without a shadow of a doubt that's what *he* wants. That he wants *me*, chooses *me*.

Realizing that if I really mean what I'm thinking, then it's over. Tomorrow, one way or another, I will get a resolution. The notion is strangely comforting, and I finally, mercifully start to feel the lull of sleep settling over me.

But not before I take myself in hand and jerk off to all the delicious sights I witnessed tonight. Blowing my load exorcises the last of my concerns, and after a quick mop-up, I sigh in contentment, drifting into the abyss.

Whatever happens in the morning, I'll know the truth.

And the truth will set you free.

CHAPTER 19

Kadence

It wasn't a dream.

It was all real.

I lie in bed the next morning feeling utterly exhausted and emotionally wrung out...but also happy in a way I've never known before. That scene was something else, and it was all because of Rafferty.

I've done group sex in the past. That's no big deal. But Rafferty held me and watched me and adored me the entire time. It's like I was the center of his universe.

And I liked it. I wanted it.

This isn't make-believe any more. It hasn't been for quite some time. I know he was clear this could only ever be a secret, short-term affair. But I knew at my door last night he was looking at me and silently asking for more.

Another kiss? To spend the night in my bed? I don't know. I was too overwhelmed, and pulled back before we could stumble any farther into choppy waters. The kiss complicated things enough for one evening.

It's kind of ridiculous that's the case, but here we are. Wild sex party? No big deal? One relatively chaste kiss?

Disaster.

Sighing, I drag my weary bones out of bed and force myself into a hot shower. It's the right move, and I start feeling better immediately. Physically, anyway. Mentally, my thoughts are still all over the place.

The kiss will only be a disaster if it ruins everything. Technically, we didn't officially agree not to do that. It was my unspoken rule that Rafferty followed, like a gentleman. So the only person here I've really compromised is myself.

But that's true of everything right now, isn't it? Rafferty doesn't know I approached him at that party to try and destroy his family's reputation. He has no idea he's a pawn in my vendetta against his son. It's only myself that I'm letting down.

So that's it. As the water cascades over my body, I blink.

I can decide the deception is over. So it *is* over.

I'm done with revenge. What's the point? It won't make me happy.

Not like Rafferty does.

My smile is shy, even though there's no one there to see it, not even myself. But I giggle like a little kid, the realization slowly washing over me.

Rafferty makes me happy. And I think I make him happy, at least to a certain extent. I understand that his life probably doesn't have room for me in it in a long-term sense. Whatever we have, though, I've decided it's just about that now, nothing else.

I release my animosity for Logan McKenna into the universe, banishing him from my soul. In fact, I feel *grateful* in a perverse way. Without him, I probably never would have thrown myself at Rafferty. I might have noticed him at that party, sure, but I highly doubt I would have pursued him so aggressively.

Even if this affair is over in a few weeks—days—*today*—

the change within me will always be there. I've learned so much not only about myself and my kink but also about what I want from anyone who I allow to be close to me again.

I owe Rafferty so much. I owe Logan nothing. I don't ever have to see him again if I don't want to, at least not on purpose. I certainly don't ever have to tell him what I shared with his father.

My vendetta is officially dead and buried.

Now back to that kiss.

I kill the shower and shake off the excess water before reaching for my towel. "Fuck," I whisper out loud. What *do* I want to do about the kiss? Make a big deal? Pretend like it never happened? If only I knew how Rafferty felt…

The only way to find that out is to have a conversation like adults. That right there is such a big difference between him and his son. Logan wouldn't even entertain the notion of admitting to *himself* that he's into men. I'm not going to tell anyone their sexuality. But that boy is one hundred percent not straight, whether he likes it or not. Yet I knew there would never be the opportunity to talk to him about it.

With Rafferty, it's not like that. He might still be kind of surprised by his attraction to me, but he's not fighting it. He might not want to shout it from the rooftops, but we weren't exactly private last night. We're taking it slowly. He's curious. It's a beautiful thing to witness.

He approaches so much in his life like that. He's open to discussion. He doesn't throw up brick walls at every turn. I feel safe with him.

And there it is. The real crux of the matter. Stanley was so quick to commit to dating, to talk about the future, but it was all just hot air. His words weren't worth anything. Rafferty has been careful not to promise me anything he can't give me. His actions, however, have spoken volumes this entire time.

Even when I broke down or pushed him away, he was there for me. He never wavered. He's created space so I could blossom, and I've grown in ways I never thought possible. Even if the kiss has irrevocably changed things, I want to show him my gratitude.

So I do it the best—and arguably only—way I know how.

Until now I hadn't had much of a reason to pay attention to the fancy dresses he gifted me. Apart from last night, I'd only been wearing outfits for Rafferty around the house. And I'm still only going to be dressing for him, but I feel possessed with my mission.

I came here to be his doll. It's time he saw the princess version. Maybe that way, whenever we go our separate ways, he'll always have an image of what he meant to me. A physical manifestation of how he made me feel.

It feels a little weird at ten o'clock in the morning to be pulling ballgowns out of the closet, but I don't care. This feels like one of those now-or-never sorts of situations. Licking my lips, I consider my options. There's that Jane Austen-looking one, but it's a bit chaste for this occasion, I think. After all, I'd quite like this declaration of feelings and intentions to end with a raw and passionate fucking.

Ahhh. Perfect.

Because I hadn't removed this particular dress before, I didn't realize that it's actually a dip hem skirt. That means it's short at the front and long around the back. The lilac tulle is almost like a ballerina's tutu, so voluminous I already know it's going to be a riot to wear and flounce around the house.

I touch the beaded top half with a sweetheart neck, marveling that it's not constructed for someone with breasts —or at least, only meant to accommodate small ones. I do still have pecs, after all. Rafferty really did just go a thousand percent 'I fucked a boy and I liked it' when he was picking out this wardrobe. His lack of freakout really was—and still is—refreshing.

Of course I'm not going for demure here. I slip a purple, lacy jock strap on and find my white, bedazzled thigh-high boots with the four-inch heels that could pierce a man's heart. Kiki might be in princess mode today, but she's also still a ho.

Again with the contradictions, I select the extravagantly constructed floral necklace to wear, the range of different colored gems sparkling like a fresh rainbow at the base of my throat. I add a pink tennis bracelet around my wrist as well as a drop earring made from spiraling platinum strands, diamonds, and pink sapphires.

Perfect.

I take time applying my face. I get the feeling that Rafferty is going to give me space this morning after what happened last night, so unlike usual, I'm not anxious about him bursting in.

I go full out with a complicated design around my eyes. Not my lips, though. I'm hoping I'll be getting some use out of them soon enough. A simple shade of lipstick does the trick, but my eyes have several colors, multi-layered liner, sparkles, and even some little stick-on pearl details around the outsides, just for fun. Finally, I don a pair of white lacy fingerless gloves that add an extra touch of glam.

When Rafferty sees me, I want him to know that he makes me feel like a queen. Like the star of the show. The belle of the ball.

I want him to know that *I* know that I'm the doll that rocked his world and changed his life.

Just like he changed mine.

Feeling like Miss USA, I rise to my feet, ready to sweep my Daddy off his feet. It occurs to me that he's probably been the one making decisions and providing for people most of his life. He's taken care of me like no other. But I swore to cater to his every whim, to worship him, to give him an escape.

It's time to turn that promise up to the max.

As I open my door, I listen keenly. Not hearing anything, I venture into the hallway, sparing a glance toward his room, but deciding that even if in the unlikely event that's where he is, I don't want to go there uninvited again. That was a raw and vulnerable moment for the both of us.

That isn't the vibe today.

I'm afraid but excited as I strut down the stairs, my fuck-me boots clicking on the wooden floor, thinking he might be in his office. I wonder if he's in a meeting. Camera on or off? Would I disturb him either way? I could just straddle his lap in my beautiful gown and show him how much last night meant to me with all his staff 'watching' again.

The noise of the front door shutting pulls me from that daydream, though. Rafferty must have popped out. Sometimes he likes to drive for the sake of it if it's a nice morning or go out for coffee and bagels despite always having a fully stocked kitchen. Perhaps he had deliberately gone out to give me that space we both know I needed. Or he wanted to drive around and clear his head.

Whatever the case, he's back now.

And I'm ready for him.

Grinning from ear to ear, I swish my way toward the entrance hall, spinning around the corner like a Hollywood starlet who's ready for her close-up.

"Ohh, Daddy," I coo as I turn. "I've been waiting for you, and I'm so very desperate for your big, fat co—"

The words die in my throat as my eyes widen and panic grips my chest.

It's not Rafferty who's standing there, staring at me in horror with a dropped jaw.

It's his son.

CHAPTER 20

Rafferty

I smirk to myself as Kadence's voice floats through from somewhere near the front of the house into the kitchen, where I'd been sipping coffee. I hadn't wanted to disturb him this morning, wanting him to come to me. He's been waiting for his Daddy, has he? That suits me just fine.

Except someone else replies to him. There's someone else in the house.

Someone I've known his whole life.

"What the ever-loving *fuck* are you doing in my home, Hughes?" Logan shrieks.

I'm not even sure if when I slam my coffee down on the counter that it stays upright. I'm too busy sprinting toward the sound of their voices. I skid to a halt in the entrance hall. It could have been comical if either of them had been looking my way instead of fixating on each other. However, Logan looks like he's going to punch the nearest wall, and Kadence is possibly going to pass out.

Which is a shame because he looks like an actual *dream* right now. A shimmering cloud of lilac and jewels but with just enough radiant skin showing it makes me want to throw him down to the floor and ravage him there and then.

"I-I—" Kadence stammers.

Logan notices me first, his surprise becoming fury. "What the hell is this little fag doing here, Dad? And why is he…why would he…" I see the moment the penny drops. Logan staggers back a couple of steps, clenching his fists. "Who's 'Daddy'?" he croaks.

I take a breath, collecting my thoughts and looking at Kadence. His expression is wretched, and it takes everything I have not to run to him and gather him tightly in my arms. But I absolutely have to do some damage control first.

This timing couldn't be worse. The very morning that my boy and I need to have a thorough heart-to-heart about where our relationship stands, Logan shows up out of nowhere and throws himself right in the middle of everything.

Fuck.

"I wasn't expecting you, son," I say calmly, stepping closer and slipping my hands into my pockets. Kadence looks like a rabbit who's been caught in someone's high beams, and instead of running, he's frozen solid, just waiting to be crushed into the asphalt.

"No shit, Sherlock!" Logan exclaims, thrusting his hands out. His frantic gaze flicks between Kadence and me. "Someone needs to tell me what the fuck is going on right the fuck now. What is this little shit doing in my house? And why does he look like *Stripper Barbie?*"

"I think he looks beautiful," I say, throwing Kadence my warmest smile. It takes a second, but his eyes finally tear away from Logan to look at me. Like it's taken an extra ten seconds for him to process my words, he sags in relief, offering me a small smile.

I nod subtly his way. He does the same back.

When I turn my attention back to my son, I'm genuinely concerned that he might be having an aneurysm.

"I—you—him—what— FUCK!"

I raise my hands and inch closer, like I'm trying to soothe a wild animal that's so frightened it's becoming violent. I don't doubt that something truly appalling is going to make its way out of my son's mouth any minute now. I don't care if it's directed at me, only if he's going to try and hurt Kadence.

But then…my own penny drops.

Logan knows Kadence by his full name.

"Have you two met before?" I ask cautiously.

Logan's scoff tells me everything. "Yeah, we went to college together. That's not the million-dollar question here, *Dad.* Why is this cross-dressing little freak calling you 'Daddy'? *Why is he in our home?*"

I shrug. "It's my home, son. You have your own place. We weren't expecting you."

"We?!" he shrieks. He runs his hand down his face, then shakes his head at me before scowling at Kadence. "One of my buddies heard on the grapevine that my old man was getting frisky at a party last night with some kind of he/she." He snaps his attention back to me. "I told them they were full of shit and came over to hear you tell me it wasn't true. And I find *this?* What is going on?!"

Fury surges through me. How dare he use that slur against my boy. Not to mention, those events are supposed to be confidential. Best believe I will be contacting the organizers as soon as possible to register my complaint and strongly suggest they vet their guest list better next time.

But what's done is done. The cat is out of the bag as much as I've been forced out of the closet. This is happening without Kadence and me getting the chance to even discuss how *we're* feeling.

Oh, well. I was always planning on leaving my heart on my sleeve and being honest about my intentions.

First, I deflect for a moment, needing more information. "I wasn't aware that you two knew each other."

I shoot a questioning look at Kadence, but he's staring at the floor, vibrating all over, his hands clenched together. I can't read him, so I move on. He doesn't have to say anything he doesn't want to in front of my son anyway.

There's no point in lying. We might not have openly discussed it, but I'm certain that Logan is fully aware that his mother and I see other people. He's not going to be the kind of child that weeps if Mommy and Daddy get divorced.

No. His horror has many layers, but that's not one of them.

"Kadence and I did meet at a party—a few weeks ago. We made a connection. He's very dear to me. I asked to spend more time with him, and he's been staying in the spare room."

Logan just frowns for a moment before wagging his finger at me. "But you are *fucking* him, correct?"

I raise my eyebrows in a warning. "There's no need to be vulgar to my guest."

Logan presses his fingers to his temples and sort of lurches around in a circle before addressing me again. "But you're *straight*."

I shrug nonchalantly. "Apparently not." *Beauty is beauty*, I think to myself.

"With him! Of all people. Dad! Wait…"

I narrow my eyes at my son. "What is that supposed to mean," I say, my voice dangerously low. What the hell does he have against Kadence? I don't like his tone at all. Jesus, did Logan bully him or something?

But I don't think he's listening to me. He's still wagging his finger my way, a frown on his forehead as he concentrates. "Wait…*wait.* Did you approach him…or did he approach you?"

"How is that any of your business?" I ask.

Logan's jaw drops, and he lets out a hollow laugh. Kadence has been conspicuously quiet this entire time. Even now, he looks like he just wants to disappear. Where's my feisty young man gone? If he and Logan do have a history, why isn't he fighting back? Out of respect for me? The urge to go to him is even stronger, but my feet are still rooted to the spot.

Logan slaps his hand over his eyes and laughs again, louder and meaner. "Oh my fucking god. He approached you. He seduced you. He made you *gay.*"

"No one can make anyone change their sexuality," Kadence hisses, finally piping up. "We're all born that way. Lady Gaga had a whole song about it. Or have you been so deep in the closet you didn't hear it?"

Ah. So Kadence knows Logan well enough to realize he's in desperate, toxic denial. I suppose he maybe didn't want to risk outing Logan against his will, so that's why we never discussed it. Still, I feel a little hurt. My son and I have been drifting apart for years, but I still love him. And Kadence…

Well, I certainly care for him a lot.

A *lot.*

The idea that they know each other is perturbing. But seeing the rage coming from Logan right now—not to mention the fear and hurt from Kadence—is far from ideal.

It's hard not to feel vindicated by Logan's reaction to Kadence's words about people not being able to choose their sexuality. He's clearly furious at me for my deception or betrayal or whatever he views it as. But I can't imagine how he's feeling about himself. His internalized homophobia is worse than I imagined, or so it seems.

I'm trying to be generous toward my soon-to-be ex-wife.

But in that moment, a wave of furious anger crashes over me. This is her fault—hers and her whole prejudiced family. My son would never be this messed up if it wasn't for them.

But he might not be this bad if I'd fought harder for him as well. I suppose I just didn't think it would be much of an issue for him until it was obviously too late. He never should have been fed these damaging ideas, either way.

Logan doesn't seem to hear Kadence's words of wisdom, sadly. He's too busy laughing. It gets so loud it begins to feel like hysteria. Concerned, I reach out for him, but he shoots backward like my touch would burn him. When he looks at me, all mirth is gone.

"He picked you up on purpose to fuck with me, you know that, right?"

Coldness prickles my flesh, but I merely raise my eyebrows at him before glancing at Kadence.

My beautiful boy's perfect face has gone the color of day-old oatmeal.

"Oh?" I say.

Logan is pacing, shaking his head, pulling at his hair. "This is what you meant by revenge, Hughes? This is how you were going to get me back? By *fucking my father*? To what end? Did you think it would make me apologize to you? How were you going to...?" It's my son's face that loses its color now. "Holy shit. Do you have photos or videos or something? You sick fuck! What were you going to do? Tell me!"

I look at Kadence, realization dawning on me.

Oh...no...

"This was all a scheme?" I ask, not sure how I feel about the matter.

Kadence's lip trembles, and my heart comes close to imagining how it would feel if it broke. Not for anything he may or may not have done. Because he looks so utterly broken, and I can't stand it.

"I'm so sorry," he whispers.

"I *knew* it!" Logan gloats, punching the air. "You twisted little freak. You messed around with my dad to try and blackmail him to get to me! I am calling the police right now. You won't get away with this!"

He actually pulls his phone out of his pocket. However, I thrust my hand out with such force that he pauses.

"Kadence, talk to me," I say. I'm looking only at him now.

Twin tears spill down his face, and even then, he's still beautiful. "I wasn't going to hurt you, Rafferty," he rasps. "Not now. I…"

"But that was your plan, right?" Logan presses. "That's why you forced your way into my dad's life. So you could expose and ruin him, his company, our family, and me. *Right?*"

Kadence's chest is fluttering like a hummingbird as he tries to catch his breath. "Is that true?" I ask. I can't deny that my ego is bruised. I don't like being manipulated. But that's not what I see when I'm looking at my boy right now.

His face is etched with regret. "It was my plan, yes…" he utters. "But not…I wasn't going to…" He shakes his head, and his face crumples as he spins on his heel and races up the stairs, presumably toward his room. I want to chase after him more than anything, but I have to make sure that my idiot son doesn't do anything unforgivable first.

Or should I say…anything *more* unforgivable?

"Put your phone away," I snap, feeling a smug satisfaction as he does as he's told.

Christ, I've done him dirty. I let his mother mollycoddle him along with her parents, and all they've done is poison and weaken him. But it's not too late. I'm still his father, and I can still help him. Steer him right. Mend his ways.

"Why would Kadence need to exact revenge on you?" I ask calmly.

For just a second, terror flashes across his face, and I get all the information I need. "Dad, you're a victim here!" he cries. "He's...catfished you or something. Let me call the cops!"

I don't even try to stop myself from rolling my eyes. "Why do I think you don't even know the definition of catfishing? I ask again. *Why* would Kadence feel the need to get one back on *you?*"

Logan shakes his head and steps away. "You're crazy. I don't know what you're trying to imply, but—"

I laugh humorously. "Look up the definition of gaslighting while you're at it," I murmur. "It's okay. It's really not hard to work it out. You two were involved. You hurt him—presumably in some way thanks to your tragic denial of who you really are—and Kadence thought he could ruin our family name by catching me in a compromising position. Close?"

Logan's mouth opens and closes a couple of times. "N-no. What? That's not...this right here has *nothing* to do with me!"

"Hmm," I say, already turning and making my way up the stairs after my boy. "Let yourself out, please. Next time, text before you intend on visiting. There's no telling *what* that traitorous little minx and I might be up to in 'your' home."

"What?" he splutters from behind me. "Dad, you can't be serious. You're not that stupid!"

I pause and glance over my shoulder. "You're right. I'm not. Now get out. You've done enough damage already."

The moment stretches out so long as I climb another couple of steps that I think he might actually be doing as he's told. Then...

"Are you really picking him over me?" he asks in a pathetic voice.

But that's his fault if he's forgotten I'm an absolute

bastard. He brought this on himself when he made my Kiki doll cry.

This time, I don't even look around.

"On this occasion? Yes."

I don't hang around to see if he goes or not.

My sweet boy needs his Daddy.

But when I get to his room, he's gone.

CHAPTER 21

Kadence

DESPITE BEING BLINDED BY TEARS, I MOVE AT LIGHTNING speed. Before I even get to my room, the dress is unzipped, and as soon as I reach the threshold, I stop, yank it off, and toss it onto the bed along with the lacy gloves. The boots are kicked off, then I lurch for the drawers, pulling out the first pair of jeans and a T-shirt I lay my hands on. I don't bother with socks. I just shove my ankle boots on my feet, then grab my suitcase.

The only thing I really care about is my make-up. Luckily, everything is stored in one large cosmetics bag, so I put that in the case first before running to the bathroom to rescue my expensive skincare products.

Once they're packed away, I snatch up the shoes I brought with me. As Rafferty bought me so many clothes, most of mine are still tucked away in the case, unused. I just give a cursory look around the room, snatching up a couple of things I see are mine.

Then I zip up the case and run with it to the balcony.

The McKennas are still in the entrance hallway, so there won't be any fleeing out that way. But I had idly noticed the flower trellis outside my window a while ago. It was back in the beginning, when I thought if Rafferty uncovered my secret, then this might make a good escape route.

After the first few days, I never thought I'd actually have to use it. Certainly not now.

How much can change in a blink of an eye.

Throwing my case down onto the grass first, I don't hesitate as I swing off the balcony, gripping onto the wooden lattice until I steady myself. Then I scurry down to the ground from the second floor, crushing flowers and vines under my fingers and shoes as I go.

I jump the last few feet, landing reasonably upright. My plan had just been to run through the woods, then use my phone to navigate and walk home. Maybe order an Uber once I'm far enough away from the house. I don't want to risk hailing one now and waiting around where either of the McKennas can find me.

Shame threatens to well up inside me, but I shove it down. Adrenaline is helping me focus, thankfully. There will be time to cringe at my appalling actions later. Right now, I need to move.

It seems for once that luck is on my side.

There's a car parked outside. I can see from the sticker on the windshield that it's an Uber.

I don't think. I just make a beeline for it.

"Hi," I say cheerfully to the driver as I open the passenger door. "Logan said I could take this ride to get home. He's going to order another one."

The driver is an older man in his fifties or sixties who blinks slowly at me, clearly not really giving a shit. "Okay," he says with a sigh, waving at me to get inside. "He already paid me anyway. I was just waiting for another ride in this area."

Score. In no time at all I've opened my own app and booked him for myself. Easy peasy. Once that's sorted, I sag in relief, shoving my case in first—not wanting to mess around with putting it in the trunk. Then I hop inside, slam the door, and buckle up.

Several emotions wash over me at once. I drop my head in my hands and take a few deep breaths in and out to try and regain my composure. In a moment of masochism, I turn and look over my shoulder at Rafferty's house one last time.

Just in time to see Logan come storming out of it.

Oops. Well…I guess that can be my revenge instead.

A sob threatens to claw out of my chest at my gallows humor. I swallow it down and ignore the inquisitive look from the driver. When his eyes are back on the road, I stare at the trees until they drop away as we join the highway that will lead me back to Paddle Creek.

Where I belong.

This whole endeavor has been one giant mistake after another. I never should have concocted such a harebrained scheme. Logan's words hurt, and the humiliation of crying in front of everyone felt like something I could never get over.

But I would have.

I was just so caught up in the moment. It felt like I was dying. After the neglect from my parents and Stanley, it felt like I was never going to be loved for who I was, so why bother?

The sad, pathetic truth was that the reason Logan's words cut me so deep was because they were true. I act like nothing matters to me, but I want to matter to someone more than *anything*.

I think I found that with Rafferty. I mattered to him.

And now it's all gone.

Somehow, I manage to hold it together until the guy drops me off. He might not have been the friendliest driver, but I really appreciated some quiet time to myself just now, so I give him five stars and a decent tip. It's all a blur as I rush into my building, up the elevator, and into my apartment.

"Hello!" I yell, belatedly realizing that I should have warned Erika first in case she and her girl were in a scene in the middle of the living room or something. It is a Saturday, after all. But my way is mercifully clear as I hurry toward my bedroom, hurtling inside and not even bothering to close the door as I collapse onto my bed.

After that, there's no holding the sobs back. They quickly become howls.

"Kadence?" Erika's voice comes from the doorway.

"I'm fine," I mumble into my pillow.

"Yeah, you look just peachy," she drawls. After a second, I feel the mattress dip, and her hand rests on my back. "Do you want to tell me what happened?"

"No," I say petulantly.

She laughs. I can practically feel her shaking her head. "Okay, tough guy. Then you won't mind me texting for reinforcements, will you?"

I'm not sure what she means by that. But in the ensuing quiet, I concentrate on breathing, willing the tears to stop leaking into my pillow.

Eventually, Erika's stubbornness pays off. "I fucked up," I say.

She hums. "The old man you were using for revenge found out you were blackmailing him and his son?"

Sighing, I finally turn my head and look at her. She's got shorts and a button-down on, complete with suspenders and her sensible glasses. It doesn't appear like she was in the middle of a scene, for which I'm grateful.

"Worse," I croak.

"Worse?" she repeats.

I nod. "I fell in love with him. *Then* he found out I was planning on betraying him."

"Oh, baby," she says sadly, combing her fingers through my hair.

"I wasn't going to humiliate him, though," I tell her, desperate for her to believe me, to understand. "Not anymore. I swear."

She shakes her head. "I seriously doubt you would have *ever* done that, sweetie. So why are you here instead of talking it through?"

I screw my face up, shaking my head before hiding away against the pillow again. "It's over," I wail, my body shaking once more with grief. "I'm a terrible person! I ruin *everything!*"

She continues rubbing my back. "That's not true, Kay," she says softly. "You're amazing. You made a stupid choice, but you didn't actually follow up with it. You worked it out before any damage was done."

"Rafferty hates me," I mumble. That's the worst damage I could imagine.

She takes a breath as if she's going to reply. A childish part of me wants her to tell me that's not true, even though I know it is. But there's a knock at the door. "Ah. That sounds like the cavalry." She pats my back, and I feel her get off the bed.

The last thing I want is to see any of my friends right now. But it seems like it's out of my hands, so I surrender to the inevitable. Luckily, I keep a box of tissues by my bed, so I pluck one out and do my best to dab at my eyes. I'd forgotten about all the glamorous make-up I did, but hopefully I don't look too much like Clayton, the college campus raccoon.

I take a couple of breaths and rub my chest. It's then I realize the other thing I'd forgotten. I'm still wearing Rafferty's jewelry. The necklace, bracelet, and earring—everything. Fresh horror rises inside me. I didn't mean to steal them! I'll have to mail them back—even though it pains me. I'd love to keep a memento of our time together, but that's just not possible. Not after the way I let him down.

The thought of Rafferty being back in that house, reevaluating every single moment of our time together, and realizing it was all a scam makes me sick to my stomach. I want to crumble all over again, but the murmured voices by the door stop, and I hear footsteps approaching. Taking a deep breath, I'm determined not to be a complete mess for my friends.

Sure enough, Erika comes back into my room, followed by Jessie and Harper, both of them looking anxious. Jessie's wearing his Kittens training gear. He must have been on his way to cheer practice.

"You guys didn't need to come," I say sheepishly with a sniff.

Jessie and Harper share a look. "Erika said it was an emergency, so yeah, we did," Harper explains.

"But, um," Jessie adds nervously. "We ran into someone else in the hall. He said he had to speak to you."

They move aside...and then there's Rafferty, standing right in front of me.

I squeak, unable to do much else.

"We'll, uh, give you guys some space," Erika says, ushering my friends out. I just stare at Rafferty until I hear the front door open and close, signaling that we have the apartment to ourselves.

"How did you find me?" I blurt out.

He chuckles ruefully and shakes his head. "You're my employee, remember?"

My face burns. No, I had quite forgotten that. "I'll pay the money back," I mumble, unable to meet his eyes.

"Why would you do that?" he asks. His calm demeanor is killing me.

I wince and hug my knees to my chest. He's just standing

over me as I try and do my best to disappear. But he's between me and the door, so escape isn't going to be as easy this time around.

"You know why," I rasp. "I tricked you. It was all a lie."

"Was it?"

"Yes!" I snap, finally glaring right into his eyes, fresh tears falling down my face. "Weren't you listening to Logan? It was all a plot to get revenge on him for humiliating me. For him never once treating me with respect despite all the times I let him fuck me. For him treating me like I was *nothing*."

For a moment, Rafferty is still. Then he nods and goes and sits on the chair at my desk, facing me, his hands clasped between his knees. "And how were you going to do that? Do you have photos of the two of us in compromising situations? Videos? Sound recordings? Did you have someone spying on us at the party last night? Or when we met?"

I swallow and shake my head. "No," I say softly. "That was the plan, but..."

"But you didn't actually go through with any of it," Rafferty says. I don't understand what he's saying. But I realize he's right about one thing.

"You were paying me," I say.

"Yes," he agrees. "As a personal assistant. Were you going to prove that wasn't your job?"

"I could have," I say with a shrug, looking away again.

"But you didn't?" he prompts. "Are you going to?"

I shake my head more vigorously, squeezing my eyes shut as more tears leak out. "No, I swear!" I cry pitifully. "I wasn't going to do anything. I wasn't ever going to tell you. I-I changed my mind."

He sighs. "Then pardon my confusion, Kadence, but what the hell's the problem here?"

"I *used* you!" I yell at him, angry that he's making me spell out my failings so cruelly. "I knew who you were that first night, and I seduced you to try and ruin your family name so I could get revenge on my heartless fuck buddy! I lied! I took advantage of your very real bisexual awakening! I am nothing but scum and Logan is right—you *should* report me to the police!"

My words hang in the air for quite some time as I pant. We stare at each other.

"Do you want me to be disappointed?" Rafferty asks.

"Yes!" I reply incredulously.

He nods once. "Fine. I'm disappointed that my son hurt you. He's going to have to work very hard to earn my forgiveness on that one. I'm disappointed you left without allowing us any time to talk through not just the events of this morning but also what happened last night. I'm disappointed that you scared me when I searched the house and couldn't find you. I'm disappointed that my boy still seems to be in that bed and not wrapped in his Daddy's arms *where he belongs.*"

He actually looks a little pissed off by the time he finishes speaking. I blink, trying my best to digest his words.

"W-what?" I say eloquently.

He huffs. "Are you disobeying your Daddy, Kadence?"

I'm still too confused, though. "Why would you want anything to do with me now? It was all a sham."

He tilts his head and raises his eyebrows. "Everything we shared was a sham?" he says in a clarifying tone. "Every scene we did was a lie? You were trying to find ways to film me that whole time, especially when we fucked in front of a literal camera and could have been discovered by my entire board of directors? You stayed beyond the weekend just to have more time to entrap me? You dressed up like a princess this morning just to get another one over on me?"

I bite my lip. "No," I utter softly.

"No, what?"

I'm trembling. Even shoving my hands under my thighs doesn't stop them from shaking. "No…none of that is true."

He grunts in satisfaction. "So I'm right in thinking that the only nefarious thing you really did was see me at the party, realize you might have an opportunity to take some power back from my son, and then seize it?"

I lift one shoulder in a partial shrug. "It was a shitty thing to do."

"It was tactical," Rafferty corrects. "You saw me as an enemy. I admire your ingenuity."

Baffled, I stare at him. "You do?"

It's his turn to shrug. "Yes. But I guess it also depends on something."

"What?" I ask immediately, desperate for a shred of redemption.

He studies me a second, and I hope a hundred times harder that my make-up isn't dripping down my face. "How do you see me now? Am I still your enemy?"

"No," I groan. The tears flow once more as I grimace and shake my head. "No, of course not. I…I…I don't want to hurt you. I'm so sorry for everything I've done. This is all such a mess!"

"The only mess is how this all unfolded today," Rafferty says practically. "That wasn't my intention, obviously. I wanted to discuss how you were feeling, but I can see that might be complicated. So let me be straight with how I'm feeling." He smirks. "Okay, maybe straight isn't the right word."

I'm aware my mouth is hanging open. I thought he was furious, that he hated me. I'm not sure what's happening right now, but so long as he's still talking, he's not leaving. I nod, urging him to continue.

"This isn't a fling for me, Kadence," he says as he leans his elbows on his knees, looking earnestly at me. "I care deeply for you. I think I might even love you. The light you've brought into my life is incomparable. You've awakened sexual desires in me I never knew existed. But it's not simply that. Your presence in my home is calming. Sweet. Delightful. And yet still sassy and enticing. I am as content watching TV with you cuddled up by my side as I am fucking my gorgeous Kiki doll until we both come our brains out. I don't want you to leave. If you agree, I don't want to hide you away, either. It's true that I'm afraid of how you might be treated by others, but I'm not afraid of coming out for you. Of telling the world that you're mine. I'll be your Daddy, your partner, whatever you want. But I do need to know what you want, preferably soon. Not because I need to tell my wife or my son or my staff. But because if I don't know how you really feel right this minute, I might just die."

He swallows, his eyes glassy as he stares at me, his gaze unblinking, holding his breath as he waits for my answer.

It's too much. I can't fight this battle any longer. I feel myself break down as a sob wracks my chest. *"Daddy!"* I cry, launching from the bed and throwing myself into his arms.

He gathers me in his lap, hugging me fiercely as I wrap my legs around his waist and my arms around his back, burying my face into his neck. "Shh, shh," he soothes me, stroking my hair.

"I love…I want…" Nothing I need to say is coming out of my mouth.

"You can have whatever you want, Kadence," he assures me. "You can move in. You can be my doll, my boyfriend. I'm all in. I know this isn't just an experiment anymore. It never really was, I don't think. I want to give a real relationship a go. If you'll have me."

I lean back incredulously. "If *I'll* have *you?*" I splutter. He raises his eyebrows, and I realize he's serious. "You trust me?"

His shoulders drop just a fraction, and he smiles sweetly

at me. "You might have neglected to mention a couple of things, sweetheart. But I don't believe you ever actually lied to me. Not with your body or your soul."

I shake my head. He might have a point there. "It started out as something else, but everything I felt was true."

He brushes back a curl. "I know, beautiful boy. Why else would you have lost your temper with me like that about your town? That argument wasn't anything to do with our relationship beyond us both realizing how much we care what the other thinks of us. You showed me your heart for real that night. I know who you are. I do trust you. I want to be with you. I want to build something new together."

I close my eyes. It seems impossible that I have any more tears left to cry, but these feel different than before. They are my relief, my joy.

"I want that too, Daddy," I manage to whisper, opening my eyes again. "I want to be your boy and your doll. I want to stay with you. I want to go public with you, but only when you're ready for that. I...I love you, Rafferty. So much. No one has ever come close in my life to getting me like you do. You're kind and thoughtful and sexy and commanding. I love it all."

We only look into each other's eyes a second before we lean in together, our lips meeting for the second time. Last night I was drunk on endorphins, strung out from sex, and high on adrenaline.

Right now, I am clear-headed. I know this is the only thing in the whole world I want. I am committed to whatever bumpy road lies ahead. So long as I have Rafferty by my side, I can do anything.

He sighs against my mouth and breaks the kiss, rubbing my back and gazing into my eyes. "What do you say, my beautiful boy? My perfect doll. Shall we go home?"

"Home," I repeat with a shaky laugh. He really means it this time. He wants it to be *our* home now.

It's not like we're out of the woods yet. We have a lot more obstacles still to overcome. But as he takes me by the hand and picks up my suitcase, I let all those worries fade away. We can deal with them later.

In this moment, all we need is each other.

CHAPTER 22

Rafferty

I can't lie. Discovering Kadence's room looking like a crime scene almost stopped my heart. I tore through the house looking for him, but it didn't take long for me to realize that he was really gone.

That had been unacceptable, to say the least.

I didn't hesitate to call Audrey on a Saturday morning in order to get Kadence's address. She knew better than to tease me or ask any questions. She was fully aware of what the deal was when I 'hired' him. She understood the significance of me needing to find him.

And find him I did.

Our declarations weren't what I'd been expecting when I woke up this morning, but damn it all to hell if they didn't mean everything to me anyway.

As it had been such short notice, I'd simply driven myself to ensure I got to Kadence as soon as possible. The downside of that is I can't hold him as I drive us back to the outskirts of Albertson. I settle for resting my hand on his thigh, his own hand covering mine as we make the short, quiet journey.

Home.

Obviously, it's not going to be a simple case of moving him in. I need to speak with Charleen as a matter of urgency. This is still technically her home, too. But I need Kadence with me now. We can work out the logistics later.

All that matters is that he's mine, really mine. There will be no more talk of 'when this ends,' because I'm in it for the long haul now, and so is he. As soon as I've briefed Charleen, I want to make our relationship public. There's no reason to sneak around anymore.

This is who I am. He is who I want.

After I park in the garage and help him inside with his case, he stands in the foyer, looking lost. He glances around, perhaps expecting Logan to pop out of the woodwork. I place my hand on the small of his back, and he immediately relaxes against my touch.

"We're alone," I assure him.

He nods. "Good. Thank you."

I don't tell him that I plan to have the locks changed as soon as possible, as I don't want to cause any more stress or drama right now. I'll tell Charleen of course and get her a new set of keys cut. But Logan is going to have to earn his right to come back in here unannounced.

Kadence asked earlier if I was disappointed. I am in my son, certainly. But I'm not giving up on him. He's still young. He's got time to sort his act out and turn his life around. But I meant what I said to him when we last spoke. If it's a choice between him and Kadence, at least for the time being, I'm choosing my sweet boy.

"Do you want to rest?" I ask him. The urge to feed him is strong. He's been through an awful shock. But he's also dead on his feet, and my overwhelming instinct is that he needs sleep. We can spend the rest of the day cozying up, and I can care for him all I want.

He nods as he looks up at me. It's amazing how well his

make-up has survived all that crying, but his eyes are still red-rimmed.

I lead him back up to his bedroom where I open up his case and find the bag with his skin care products. "Go wash your face, gorgeous. I want you to be relaxed and comfortable."

He offers me a tiny smile as he takes the bag and goes to do just that. In the meantime, I straighten up his dress and hang it back in the closet. Any drawers that had been left open, I close, and I zip up his case again so I can tuck it away in the corner for now.

When he returns, his face is plump and glowing, shining from all the moisturizers. He's left the products in the bath-room. Good. He's not going anywhere anytime soon.

"Come here," I murmur, slipping my hands against his and leading him toward the bed. It doesn't matter that it's early afternoon. I've already pulled the curtains to make it nice and dark, and this brave boy is having a nap.

Gently, I lift his T-shirt over his head, then slide his jeans down. The poor thing was in such a hurry that he didn't even put socks on before he left. He is, however, wearing a very pretty purple lacy jock-strap. He watches me as I hum and run my hands over the globes of his ass.

"Did you wear that for me today?" I ask, already knowing the answer. I just want to hear it for myself from his sweet lips.

"Yes, Daddy," he whispers.

I move my hands so one is curled around his wrist and the other rests at his throat. "I'm glad you kept these on," I tell him, referring to the jewels I gifted him. But he bites his lip and closes his eyes.

"It was an accident. I realized just before you arrived. I was going to mail them back."

It's my turn to shake my head and frown. "They're yours.

You never have to give them back, no matter what. But I would like to take them off now, if that's okay? They won't be very comfortable to sleep in."

He nods. "Yes, Daddy."

Thankful, I unclasp the necklace and the bracelet, then slip the earring out of the hole in his lobe, setting them all carefully on the dresser. When I come back beside the bed, I place my hands on my boy's hips. "Do you want something to sleep in?" I ask.

He shakes his head, and I go to push his underwear down, but his hands come up to rest on my chest, and that stops me.

"Will you stay with me?" he asks in a small voice. His words sound loud in the hush of the room, though.

"Of course," I say without hesitation.

He gives another little nod, then he slowly starts unbuttoning my shirt.

I watch as he methodically strips me down, something we've never done before. In fact, I can't think of a single instance where we had sex and I wasn't either fully or partially clothed.

Today, I let him take everything off. We don't speak as my shirt and pants drop to the floor, not even when he crouches down to divest me of my briefs. When he's done, he takes it upon himself to shirk off his jockstrap, and then there is absolutely nothing between us as we stand in front of one another.

As equals.

Silently, I pull back the duvet and lower myself onto the mattress, pulling my boy down alongside me. We naturally spoon with his back to my chest, our bodies too hot to pull the duvet back over us just now. He smells divine, and I inhale deeply as I wrap my limbs around his beautiful body.

My cock is pressed up against his thigh, and I can't help but react to his proximity. It's impossible. I'm addicted to him. I don't want to pressure him into anything after the day he's had—not to mention how sore he must be from the night before. But he moans and places his hands over mine, guiding one of them down to wrap around his length.

"Daddy," he murmurs as he looks over his shoulder, leaning to capture my mouth in a searing kiss.

"Kadence," I say against his lips. It's important to me that he knows this isn't a scene. I'm not playing with Kiki right now.

I'm making love to my boy.

With my free hand, I angle my cock and push it between his clasped thighs. A mixture of precum and sweat gives me just enough lubrication so I can slide it back and forth between his legs, leisurely using his perfect body to pleasure myself. We jerk him slowly off together as I kiss his mouth, along his jaw, and against the pulse point on his neck.

"Daddy," he pleads quietly over and over again, that one word conveying so much want and need.

"I'm here, baby boy," I tell him. "I've got you. You're safe. Just let go."

He spills over our linked hands with a little squeak and a gasp, his body shuddering against mine. I take my time as I rut between his thighs, letting my climax build naturally as he rests heavily in my arms. His eyes are closed, and he lets out a tiny moan of pleasure. It's enough to send me over the edge, and I finally empty my load over his legs.

Some of both our mess has dripped down onto the sheet. I reach for some tissue to mop us up as best I can, then simply move us away from the wet patch. I'll deal with that later. For now, it's time to fall asleep together in the same bed for the very first time.

All I care about in that moment is being with my boy. The man I love. It's terrifying to think what power he holds over my heart, but I know I'm not going to shy away from it or him. I'm going to embrace everything he has to offer. This is only the beginning of our relationship, and I hope with everything I have that it's going to be a long and beautiful one.

Kadence Hughes is mine. I protect what's mine.

Forever.

Epilogue

Three Months Later
Rafferty

"Ooh, Daddy! How about this one?"

I've given up trying to shush Kadence, despite being in a bustling crowd. If people hear him call me that, then they hear. Instead, I smile as he tugs me by the hand down an aisle of large wire cages. He's so light and carefree these days, I never want to dim his shine.

The first official Paddle Creek Summer Fair is in full swing, and honestly, I can't remember the last time I was so proud of a project. Compared to the multimillion dollar deals I used to negotiate for breakfast, this event is peanuts. But it represents something that I've become the biggest advocate for.

Change.

It's pretty crazy to think back to my life just a few months ago before I crossed paths with a certain beautiful, bratty, bossy doll. Since then, I've separated amicably from my wife and started divorce proceedings while she made her permanent move to the West Coast.

I informed my board of directors that I wouldn't be selling off my properties in Paddle Creek after all, choosing alternatively to invest in the area.

The board has had quite a few resignations and replacements since then, but somehow, my company still survives without them. They still have those dreadful fundraising events, but I haven't felt it necessary to attend one lately.

Kadence did bring me to my first drag show, though. That was quite an education. In fact, The Ice Cream Parlor is co-running the bar here today and their headliner queen, Kimmi Sugar, is giving a performance later.

O'Toole's is the other drinks sponsor here today, partnering with the local Cardinal chapter and Horowitz's garage. They're letting kids take photos on the bikes and are running demonstrations on simple motorcycle maintenance.

Food is being offered by Dino Mite, the themed kids' fast-food joint that I remember taking Logan to once when he was a kid. Staff are wearing their signature T-Rex baseball caps as they sell burgers, fries, slices of pizza, and shakes.

Some of the art students from the college are painting faces. Butterflies nail salon is selling bottles of polish and other beauty products but also applying false lashes and face jewels for free, all while blasting eighties rock music.

The Paddle Creek Kittens are soon scheduled to perform a version of their latest competition routine that they've adapted to make safe on the parking lot asphalt. We're in the shadow of the Paddle Creek Panthers football stadium, and the players are volunteering all across the fair today. I keep looking up at the building every now and again, marveling how I almost bought the whole damn thing on a whim.

I thought I knew this town. But I'd just been lording over

it. Kadence had been right. I only saw it as a business opportunity, not thinking about the real people I was hurting.

Not anymore.

Against some strong objections from certain members of my board, I helped form a coalition so that the businesses and residents of this town could have a communication network as well as a board of their own to represent their best interests. I'm no longer planning on either selling or flattening the properties I've accumulated here over the years. I'm hunting for new tenants to fill the vacant lots with exciting new prospects.

Hence the fair. It was actually Kadence who suggested that the town needed an opportunity not only to show off what it already has, but also to do some much-needed fundraising.

I was reluctant at first to introduce a charity element. I simply wanted to crack open my check book and start spending. But again, it was Kadence who patiently pointed out that wouldn't drum up much community spirit.

Gone are the days when the McKennas will be the overlords lurking in the shadows as this town slowly crumbles while it begs for refurbishment. I've been getting to know so many of the business managers but also the community figures like the school principals, religious leaders, the sheriff, and the new mayor. Paddle Creek isn't just a series of financial decisions for me anymore.

It's home.

I frequently marvel that in just a few short months this town has felt more welcoming to me than Albertson ever did. It was always Charleen who wanted to visit there. But it's become frighteningly obvious how very little we had in common toward the end of our marriage.

In fact, it's been made blindingly clear to me how little I

had in common with most of my so-called acquaintances. Once word got around that I was a 'fucking queer,' a great many of them apparently lost my number.

What a shame.

"Look, look!" Kadence cries breathlessly, pulling my gaze away from the stadium and my attention back from my deep thoughts. He looks stunning as always in denim shorts that barely skim his ass and a floaty top. My heart skips a beat whenever I look at him, like it's still the first time I'm laying my eyes on him.

"Hmm?" I say, realizing he's trying to tell me something. I look down at the rows of cages and their timid occupants, already sensing how my day is going to go.

One of Kadence's best friends is a human kitten whose Daddy runs the cat café in town, Toe Beans. They're selling coffee and cakes today, but their main purpose at the fair is an adoption drive. They worked with the local animal shelter where they foster the cats at the café to safely transport all the animals today. These kitties—and the pups in the adjacent row—are looking to find their forever homes.

I've never had a pet in my life, but Kadence seems determined that we're going to rescue a cat. As unsure as I am that's a good idea, as usual, I'm powerless to say no to my boy when he really wants something.

His attention is completely focused on reading every description attached to each cage. Plenty of the little kittens and fluffy cats have other people peering down at them, but Kadence keeps tugging me past those.

"No, Daddy," he says impatiently. "We have to check out the ones that are being overlooked!"

I sigh, thinking that it would be easier to buy a pedigree kitten from a breeder. I have no idea what to do with a cat, let alone one that's had a hard life. But I'm willing to follow Kadence's lead and see where that takes us.

He's not steered me wrong so far.

It's insane for me to think back on how our relationship began with deception. I don't believe for a minute that Kadence was ever truly intending on ruining me. I'm only sorry that he carried that secret around for so long. The bridge that still needs healing is with my son. It took a while, but Kadence talked to me about what happened and how Logan treated him.

For now, we're keeping our distance from each other. I've offered to pay for therapy, but Logan is yet to take me up on it. I hope time will heal this riff, but he's not going to be able to love anyone else until he loves himself.

A wise drag queen has taught me that.

And now I know what it truly means to love and be loved by a partner, I want that for him. He deserves to find peace, even if he's made mistakes in the past. There's nothing he can't come back from, or at least I hope so.

"Aww, look at this one, Daddy," Kadence says. He is at least trying to keep his voice down, but he's just so excited. While he waggles his fingers at a pretty ginger cat, I can't help but sneak a look at him.

How is he still just as beautiful to me as the day we met? I keep waiting for the butterflies to subside every time I look at him, but they're not going away. I wonder if they ever will. I bet in years to come he'll still be bringing light into my life.

There's no part of me that doubts he'll still be mine, no matter how far into the future I look. But there isn't any need to rush into anything for now. It's still something I find myself saying to him after that initial weekend was over.

We've got time.

He gasps, bringing my attention fully back to the present. "What's wrong?" I hiss immediately.

Kadence waves his hands, then holds a finger to his lips to

make me be quiet. Carefully, he points over to one of the end cages.

A raccoon is reaching between the bars, trying to fish their little paw into the black cat's food bowl. "That's Clayton," Kadence whispers. I don't ask how he can tell the college nuisance-slash-mascot apart from any other pest. I just trust he's right.

The raccoon curls his little paw around a fistful of kibble. The black cat was curled up in a loaf, apparently sleeping. All the potential adoptees have either blue or pink collars on to indicate their sex, so I can tell she's a she from this distance. It seems that she might have been napping, but she was still paying attention to what's hers. Clayton barely lifts the food he's stealing an inch from the bowl before the black cat suddenly leaps to her feet, shooting across to the other side of her cage, and bopping the raccoon on the nose.

Clayton hisses and drops the kibble in shock before cradling his nose. The black cat screeches at him and lifts her paw as if to punch him again. Clayton apparently decides that he can find dinner somewhere else less hazardous, and makes a break for it, disappearing between the parked cars.

I bark out a laugh as I watch the black cat saunter back to her spot in the sun. She's clearly very pleased with herself as she starts to clean her paw, as if she's a fancy lady who had to swat a commoner away from snatching her purse.

"Oh, she's trouble," I scoff.

When I look down, Kadence has the biggest puppy dog eyes I've ever seen.

"You like a challenge, though," he whispers through a devilish grin.

I raise an eyebrow. "Of all the adorable cats here, you want that sassy minx?"

It's his turn to laugh out loud before fixing me with a knowing glare. "As if that isn't your exact preference."

Damn. He's got me there.

I sigh, already knowing I'm beaten but refusing to admit defeat so easily. "Who's going to take care of her when we go on vacation?" Because you better believe Kadence already has a passport now, and I'm planning several excursions over the coming year so he can begin to see the world.

He rolls his eyes. "Jessie and Nim, of course." Yeah, he's got me there. We couldn't really ask for anyone more quali-fied. He already knows he's won and is dragging me over to the black cat's cage. "Come on, let's find out her name."

"Little Miss Kiki the Second," I quip.

Kadence slaps my arm playfully. "You know there's only *one* Kiki," he growls.

I pull him against me for a kiss on the lips. I'll never take for granted that I can do that whenever I want, whether it's with my boyfriend, Kadence, or playing with my Kiki doll. He's mine, always.

"Damn, right," I agree. "You're once in a lifetime."

His expression melts as he cups his hand against the side of my face. "Once in a lifetime, Daddy," he tells me.

Yep. And we have all the time in the world.

———

Thank you so much for reading **Kadence and Rafferty's** story! If you enjoyed their playtime adventure, please leave a review on your favorite bookish site. It makes a big differ-ence for us indie authors!

Turn the page to discover more heartwarming Daddy books by Helen Juliet/HJ Welch, including all the previous Paddle Creek Daddies books.

———

Thank you to my team!
    Cover Design: Cate Ashwood
    Cover Model: Stephen Crowe
    Cover Photographer: Graham Martin @ Menart.co.uk
    Editing: Meg Cooper
    Proof Reading: Tanja Ongkiehong
    Love & Support: Ed, Troo, Jodi, Gigi, Hubby, and our cats

PADDLE CREEK #1: HEAVEN SENT BY HJ WELCH

Two rival jocks. One adorable nerd. A bet that changes everything.

SETH

Being captain of the Paddle Creek Panthers is my life. I wouldn't care that my grades have slipped, except it could not only cost me my shot at the pros, but now the rich kid in town has wagered that if I don't graduate, I'll owe him *big* time. Can this gorgeous little freshman geek Gabe really save my degree and my reputation? All I know is that as soon as I laid eyes on him, I needed him. And I *don't* want to share.

MARTY

I've spent almost four years trying to get my captain Seth to notice me. He's hot as hell and knows how to boss a guy around, even one as big as me. To him, though, I'm just the team clown. But when he drags me into this graduation bet, it's no laughing matter. So why shouldn't this little cherub Gabe tutor me as well? In fact, I don't see why we can't share him in all *kinds* of ways. Seth is clearly a natural Daddy, Gabe thrives being doted on, and I'm happy to Daddy *and* be Daddied. Win-win, right?

GABE

Somehow, I've found myself standing up to the guy whose family pretty much owns Paddle Creek and put my neck on the line for two of the college's star players. Now we're spending every day together as I try and save their grades, and I don't know if I'm crazy but it's like they both *want* me. I've never had a boyfriend. I'm not even out to my overbearing parents. How could I choose between them…or do I actually have to when they *both* want to be my Daddies? After my life comes crashing down, it's their turn to come to my rescue. Maybe what me and these god-like men have isn't just a fling after all?

Heaven Sent is a steamy, standalone MMM romance. It's the first book in the Paddle Creek College series, where it's always the quiet ones who get up to the best kind of trouble. This book features a geek tutoring two hot jocks, two hot jocks tutoring a geek in a completely different way, a trash panda with a heart of gold, a human ice cream sundae, a revenge curse, and a guaranteed HEA with absolutely no cliffhanger.

Click here to get the Heaven Sent eBook

PADDLE CREEK #2: YES, SIR BY HJ WELCH

Two men. Two secrets. Can true love set them free?

BENEDICT

Just one more year, then I can go back to my beloved Oxford University and leave this tiny town behind me. Teaching is my passion, but I have other desires that I know would get me fired if anyone found out. The only trouble is, my new TA is pushing all my buttons and I'm not sure he even realizes what calling me Sir does to me. That's nothing, however, compared to when he starts calling me Daddy.

JACKSON

Have I got hots for teacher? Oh, yes. Messing around is off the table, though, so in a way it's safe to flirt with him and see him lose that stiff upper lip. It's not like he'd be interested in me anyway if he ever discovered what I love wearing under my clothes. Tough guys like me shouldn't like satin and lace. They shouldn't want to feel pretty. But Sir makes me feel gorgeous, and I want to be *such* a good boy for him.

***Yes, Sir** is a steamy, standalone MM romance. It's the second book in the **Paddle Creek College** series, where it's always the quiet ones who get up to the best kind of trouble. This book features two people learning they don't have to be ashamed of who they are, a sassy brat who really wants to behave, a master in the bedroom who's a caring Daddy at heart, role playing so good it could win an Oscar, and a guaranteed HEA with absolutely no cliffhanger.*

Click here to get the Yes, Sir eBook

PADDLE CREEK #3: LITTLE PLEASURES BY HJ WELCH

One jaded Daddy. One brand new boy. A fake relationship that becomes all too real.

XANDER

It's bad enough I have to move back to Paddle Creek with my awful stepmom, but now my half-brother's best friend has decided he has to look after me—even pretending to be my new boyfriend for a family wedding to keep my stepmother off my back. What Ruben doesn't know is that I've been in love with him for as long as I can remember and spending so much time with him is torture. Until it isn't. I can't believe that he's interested in me and even wants to be my Daddy, unlocking something in me I never knew was there. But when my stepmom goes too far, can I rely on Ruben to be there for me seeing as no one else in my life ever has?

RUBEN

When my life-long best friend asks me to keep an eye on his half-brother, of course I agree. Except he's a young man now, not a kid, and he's tugging at every single one of my Daddy heartstrings. Xander has just moved back into town and between finishing his degree, part-time work, and hellish stepmother, he's stressing himself into knots. It's a long time since a boy interested me, but I just want to protect Xander from the whole world. No matter the cost.

Little Pleasures is a steamy, standalone MM romance. It's the third book in the **Paddle Creek College** series, where it's always the quiet ones who get up to the best kind of trouble. This book features a Daddy introducing a boy to his inner little, the most loyal doggy best friend, a lot of dinosaurs, a heart-stopping rescue, and a guaranteed HEA with absolutely no cliffhanger. CW: Age play but no ABDL.

Click here to get the Little Pleasures eBook

quickly met our sweet baby boy who we'll do anything for. When Brady says he's found a sassy little lamb for the three of us to stalk, I'm happy to indulge him. But this broken young man swiftly captures all of our hearts, even though he says he can walk away any time. There's a difference between walking and being taken, though. Now I have the scent of a fool who's about to discover what happens when he's stolen what's *mine*.

*Four Play is a super steamy, standalone MMMM romance. It's the fourth book in the **Paddle Creek College** series, where it's always the quiet ones who get up to the best kind of trouble. This book features exhilarating primal play, one hell of a paint ball match, an obsessive ex-boyfriend, and a guaranteed HEA with absolutely no cliffhanger.*

Click here to get the Four Play eBook

emotions are tough for me. But when the perfect boy drops into my lap, how can I refuse? Rescuing strays is what I do. It's only so long that I can resist this beautiful kitten and his bubbly personality. But someone in town has it out for me and my fellow bikers, branding us troublemakers. I can't let Jessie be dragged down with me, not when it puts everything he's worked so hard for at risk. I swore I'd do anything to protect him. Even if that means letting him go.

Hell's Kitten is a steamy, standalone MM romance. It's the fifth book in the **Paddle Creek Daddies series**, *where it's always the quiet ones who get up to the best kind of trouble. This book features first-time kitten play, two broken hearts, a cheerleading championship, far too many black cats to count, enough love for nine whole lives, and a guaranteed HEA with absolutely no cliffhanger.*

Click here to get the Hell's Kitten eBook

BEARS-4-U (MULTI-AUTHOR SHARED UNIVERSE): KEEP ME BY HJ WELCH

Snowed in for a second chance at love...

BECKETT

It's been over two years since I lost my darling husband, and my best friend is taking matters into her own hands. She's signed me up to a dating app for bears and those that love them, even encouraging me to attend a weekend mixer. I go to humor her, not expecting to rescue the most adorable boy...twice. But I'm not ready to open up my heart again, am I?

LAURIE

My last Daddy was bad news. It's taken a lot of courage for me to reach out on Bears-4-U and go to this mixer, only to find that the new Daddy I've been talking to is just as awful. That's when Beckett swoops into my life like a hero in a story book. I know he's not looking for love, but I want to mend his broken heart so badly. When a scary snowstorm blows in and strands us, I trust he'll keep me safe and warm. I want to be in his life, in his bed, in his heart… forever.

Bears-4-U is a MM Daddy romance multi-author series, featuring a host of delicious Daddy pairings. The Bears-4-U dating app is all about putting Bears and Teddy Bears together for their honey-sweet HEAs. Psst, no real bears involved. Each book can be read as a standalone, but why not snuggle up with all the bears?

Click here to get the Keep Me eBook

A DADDY FOR CHRISTMAS (MULTI-AUTHOR SHARED UNIVERSE): JALEN & COLBY BY HJ WELCH

One Daddy, two boys, and the epic road trip that brings them together

ANDREAS

While selling a bunch of stuff that's been sitting in storage here in Sydney, I end up with two guys aggressively bidding on the same childhood toy. I worry I've got a fight on my hands until I realize they're actually best friends trying to buy it for each other as a Christmas gift. The solution? Simple! They live right here in the city, so I hand deliver the present for both of them to share. What's not so simple is how adorable these young men are. How gorgeous. How the more time we spend together, the more it's starting to feel like love…

JALEN

Of course I love my BFF, Colby. Duh. I moved from California to Australia for him! But I know as much as I want him to be mine, I'm a walking disaster and he needs someone better than me to take care of him. Someone like Andreas. He appears in our life like a Christmas miracle, looking after both of us like some sort of dream Daddy. It doesn't hurt that he's not only successful but crazy generous. He seems to adore spoiling us, so when he offers to take us on an amazing trip back to his home in the UK for the holidays, how can we refuse? And if we just happen to accidentally fall into bed together, would that be so terrible?

COLBY

Thanks to the power of the internet, Jalen has been there for me for years when my own family turned their backs on me. But even after we move in together, I know he just sees me as a friend. He's too fabulous, too bright and beautiful for shy little me, so I've never said a word. However, something strange starts happening the more time we spend with our new friend, Andreas. The older man gives the most amazing cuddles and can't seem to stop showering me and Jalen with gifts. Traveling to England feels like something from a fairy tale, but what's even more unbelievable is the way his eyes light up when he's with me and my best friend. Am I crazy? Could three really be the magic number?

Jalen & Colby is part of A Daddy for Christmas, a multi-author series. All the books are standalones, but each Daddy has a unique gift for his wonderful boy (or boys). Except all boys know that sometimes Santa gets it wrong, and it's going to take a very special Daddy to make it right. So why not stay and read them all?

Click here to get the Jalen & Colby eBook

Wild Ride

When Red is chased into the woods, he seeks sanctuary at his estranged grandma's house. He doesn't expect to be rescued by his older brother's best friend, the man he was always madly in love with. Could Hunter be the Daddy of Red's wildest dreams? Especially when he unlocks a secret passion of Red's for beautiful lingerie. There's still a threat lurking in the woods, though, and Hunter realises he'll do anything to protect his beautiful boy.

Three

When three shy best friends sign up to a dating app to finally get some by the end of the year, they don't expect to all fall for the same gorgeous, slightly scary-looking Daddy. The only solution? Let him choose who he wants to bed. Except he doesn't. Daddy Wolf wants to spoil each little piggy, one after another. But when danger comes calling, will their love for each other be enough to save them all?
Includes Halloween bonus scene!

Nine Lives

When Charlie suddenly finds himself homeless and penniless, he decides to sell the only thing left he owns. Himself. For the very first time. Lucky for him he stumbles across Miller, the own of a London kink club, who saves him from those who would take advantage of him. As Miller discovers his inner Daddy, he also unlocks Charlie's kitten alter-ego. But with both their families meddling, will new love be enough to keep them together?

Click here to get the Daddy's Fairy Tales eBook bundle

boyfriend Dair when he gets home from work. Hold on to your horses, Marine!

———

Troubled Waters

Bodyguard Scout Duffy doesn't know what's worse: the fact that his scorching one-night-stand, Emery Klein, is his bratty new client, or the fact that he doesn't even remember Scout. But Emery's life is in danger thanks to his out and proud charity work, and once he finally recognizes Scout, their chemistry in undeniable.

———

Homeward Bound

Swift Coal just found out he's a father, and his daughter (and her cranky cat) are coming to stay. His best friend's younger brother, Micha Perkins, has nowhere to go and a wrongfully tattered reputation. He's relieved when Swift asks him to be a live-in babysitter. He just has to hide his lifelong crush. Easy, because Swift is straight—right?

———

Bright Horizon

With sixteen years between them, baker Ben Turner and lawyer Elias Solomon have no idea their crush is mutual. But when Ben inherits his long-lost family's estate and becomes an overnight millionaire, Elias swears to protect the innocent younger man from the vultures circling him. To unravel the mystery of the inheritance, they must go to England to confront Ben's estranged relatives…and their feelings for each other.

———

Crossed Paths

Raj Bhat is done living in the shadows. It's time for him to take charge of his own destiny and tell the man he's fallen for how he really feels.

———

Midnight Sky

It's the night before New Year's Eve. Taylan Demir is all alone, and he's just lost his dog. Except when his handsome customer, Hudson Perkins, comes to his rescue, Taylan doesn't just get his dog back. He's suddenly got a hot date, and maybe someone to kiss when the clock strikes midnight.

———

Memory Lane

Angel Shields saved Jay Coal's life in high school, and Jay has secretly loved his straight best friend ever since. Now Angel's back in town with amnesia after a suspicious work accident and it's Jay's turn to rescue him. He pretends to be Angel's fiancé to see him in the hospital, but with his scrambled-up memory, Angel's not sure it's fictional after all. He just knows he loves Jay more than ever.

———

Thin Ice

Kamran's ex broke his heart, tricked him into aiding a bank robbery, and now he wants him to do one last job. There's only one way to say no: seek the protective custody of the biggest, grumpiest FBI agent ever, Lee Marshall. And pretend to be his boyfriend for a week-long family reunion in their giant mansion. Wait, what?

———

Calm Shores

Gorgeous, sophisticated Dante walks into Oliver's bar and orders… a boyfriend?! Dante needs a man to keep his mother from setting him back up with his awful, cheating ex, and Oliver is up for the challenge.

———

Fresh Snow

Emery Klein is throwing the best Christmas party ever, but his fiancé, Scout Duffy, and all their friends have something more exciting in mind.

———

Each Pine Cove book can be read as a stand alone and has its own happy ever after. But if you read the whole series, you'll see a lot of familiar faces!

Click here to get the Pine Cove eBook bundle

Click here to get the Pine Cove audio bundle

About the Author

HJ Welch is an author of contemporary MM romance series, including the international bestselling Pine Cove series. She lives just outside of London with her husband and three balls of fluff that occasionally pretend to be cats. She began writing at an early age, later honing her craft online in the world of fanfiction on sites like Wattpad. Fifteen years and over half a million words later, she sought out original MM novels to read. By the end of 2016 she had written her first book of her own, and in 2017 she achieved her lifelong dream of becoming a full-time author. When she's not writing she's usually dancing, singing, filming music videos, taking long walks, working on jigsaw puzzles, drinking prosecco, or talking about Eurovision.

She also writes contemporary British MM fairy tale adaptations as Helen Juliet.

You can contact Helen via the following:
Newsletter: https://www.subscribepage.com/helenjuliet
Website – www.hjwelch.com
Facebook Group – Helen's Jewels
Instagram – @helenjwrites
Twitter – @helenjwrites
Book Bub – @HJWelchAuthor
Facebook Page – @HJWelchAuthor